John Davidson

Perfervid

The career of Ninian Jamieson. With 23 illus. by Harry Furniss

John Davidson

Perfervid

The career of Ninian Jamieson. With 23 illus. by Harry Furniss

ISBN/EAN: 9783337057534

Printed in Europe, USA, Canada, Australia, Japan

Cover: Foto ©Raphael Reischuk / pixelio.de

More available books at **www.hansebooks.com**

PERFERVID

THE CAREER OF NINIAN JAMIESON

BY

JOHN DAVIDSON

WITH TWENTY-THREE ILLUSTRATIONS BY HARRY FURNISS

Perfervidum ingenium Scotorum

LONDON
WARD AND DOWNEY
1890

CONTENTS

PART I

THE CAMPAIGN OF NINIAN JAMIESON

PART II

THE PILGRIMAGE OF STRONGSOUL AND SAUNDERS ELSHANDER

PART I

THE CAMPAIGN OF NINIAN JAMIESON

B

CHAPTER I

THEORIES! THEORIES!

'IT is reported that Mr. Ninian Jamieson, Provost of Mintern, has succeeded in making diamonds by an entirely original process.'

On a morning in July some years ago a red-haired man noticed this announcement in a newspaper, and with more than ordinary interest, because he was seated in a train from Edinburgh for the North on his way to Mintern.

'Ninian Jamieson.' There was a quaint flavour about the name, indicating eccentricity in the bearer of it, thought the red-haired man.

'Odd people always have odd names,' he meditated ; and addressing mentally a handsome man who sat opposite, and who was the only other occupant of the compartment, he thought he heard himself saying, and admired his speech, 'Look at

Lord Monboddo. Nature formed him an eccentric, but he came into the world with the ordinary name of Burnet. Fate, however, was not to be outdone. It made him a lawyer, and a wise one too, and raised him to the bench ; and his abnormal chin, and his belief in mermaids, and satyrs, and the quadrumanous origin of man, preposterous in an advocate called James Burnet, are all reconcilable with the title. Look at Duncornet, Scarron, Suwarrow, Melancthon, Dobrowsky ! They must have been eccentric, and so is Ninian Jamieson.'

'On the other hand,' continued the red-haired man passionately, though still mentally, to himself, his face flushing with excitement, and his eyes fixed on the handsome man opposite, 'look at the great men, as far removed from eccentricity as eccentricity is from commonplace ! How their names roll out ! Cromwell, Shakespeare, Milton, Bonaparte, Nelson, Goethe ! Listen to them,' he cried aloud, overcome by his enthusiasm ; ' Hugo, Carlyle, Bismarck, Calderon, Plato, Barbarossa, Charlemagne——'

'And Ninian Jamieson,' said the handsome man, as the other paused, not having a name quite ready.

'Ninian Jamieson !' exclaimed the red-haired man. 'How, sir ! Can you read my thoughts ? '

' But you were speaking aloud.'

' Was I ? '

' Yes ; you enumerated a list of great men, and came to a stop, whereupon I suggested a modern.'

' Ninian Jamieson.'

' Yes.'

' Is he a great man ? '

' Indisputably.'

The red-haired man sat up stiffly, and examined the handsome man from top to toe. He felt abashed, for he himself was a little stubby man, and was quite aware of his inferior appearance ; whereas the other was a tall man, well proportioned, and with a very fine face.

' Do you know this Ninian Jamieson ? ' asked the little man fiercely, having recovered from his momentary confusion.

' I know him well.'

' You do ! Then,' said the little man, pointing to the newspaper, ' how can you reconcile the fact of his being a great man with the fact that he is a provost ? Is there any book published with the title " Provosts Who Were Great Men," or " Provosts Who Became Great Men " ? Sir, there is something incompatible between greatness and the provostship of a Scotch burgh. Take my word for it, men are born to be provosts just as they are born to be

great ; and just as great men are born with great
names, so those men who are intended for provosts
are born with names which have the true municipal
ring ; and I make bold to say that there is no
surname in Scotland which, in every letter of it,
bears more distinct impress of provostship than
Jamieson.'

The little man stopped, out of breath, and the
handsome man smiled blandly.

'And you will allow me to state further,' continued the little man, when he had recovered his
breath, 'that you are possibly labouring under a
common hallucination which confounds eccentricity
with greatness. As surely as a man called Jamieson
becomes, in favourable circumstances, a provost, so
surely will an individual christened Ninian be
eccentric in a high degree. I have thus stated
three theories : first, great men have always
names which sound majestically ; second, eccentric
people have always eccentric names ; third, there
are certain names towards which municipal honours
never fail to gravitate. Ninian Jamieson is an
illustration of the second and third theories, and,
negatively, of the first.'

The little man folded his arms and threw himself
back in the corner of the carriage, his red hair

standing on end, and his gray eyes radiating theories. The handsome man continued to smile blandly.

And,' said the little man, tilting forward with a new argument, 'who ever heard of a great man making diamonds?'

'It depends,' said the other quietly, 'for what purpose he makes them.'

'Purpose!' sneered the red-haired man. 'No purpose could justify a man's making diamonds.'

'How so?'

There was no idea except contradiction in the little red-haired man's head, so that he was at a loss for a moment or two to support the statement which the handsome man had queried.

'Because it can't be done,' he said at length, with triumph.

'But it has been done,' the other insisted.

'I'll believe it when I see the diamonds, and the making of the diamonds, and the stuff out of which the diamonds are made, and not till then,' said the red-haired man.

'You wouldn't take anybody's word for it?'

'I take nobody's word for anything.'

'You don't know this Ninian Jamieson, do you?'

'No.'

'Have you ever been in Mintern?'

'No; but I'm going there now.'

'Oh!' exclaimed the handsome man, with an expression of satisfaction.

'Yes. Is there anything strange in my going to Mintern?'

'Nothing; except that I'm going there too.'

'You are! Then you can tell Ninian Jamieson, provost and diamond-maker, what I think of it,' said the little man, rapidly developing a passionate hatred for this dignitary of Mintern whose name he had not heard till that morning.

'I'll not fail to do so,' said the handsome man.

' He'll be very much concerned to hear that his name indicates that he need never aspire beyond eccentricity and municipality, for he believes himself to be a great man, fit for a much higher destiny than a provostship.'

' You can tell him from me that he has reached his zenith.'

' But he's only twenty-eight.'

' That's his eccentricity. I told you ! Who but a man called Ninian could, or would, be a provost at twenty-eight ? '

' But I don't think he'll agree with your theory about names.'

' I can't help that,' said the little man with a snort, and a tremendous emphasis on the personal pronoun.

' You see,' said the handsome man, ' there are a goodly number of great men whose names have a very ordinary or even inferior sound.'

' Mention six,' burst out the little man, like a gun that had been over-loaded.

' Dante, Burns, Pitt, Stuart, Paul, Turner,' replied the handsome man, rapidly and regularly discharging the names like a six-chambered revolver.

' But, my dear sir, don't you perceive,' said the little man, very much in earnest, ' that these names can't go into the same category with those I mentioned ? Dante is perhaps on the border line ; but a line there must be, and it is better to keep the class of greatest men very select. There's the test, sir. Has the name a majestic sound ? No ? Out with it, then ; it doesn't belong to our list. It has ? Write it up in letters of gold. It's infallible. Man '—he became familiar in his zeal—' man, there's the postulate : great men have always names that sound majestically. You can't get over that. And who's this Paul ? '

'Paul, the Apostle.'

'Pardon—pardon !' cried the little man. 'No Bible characters ! no Bible characters ! And what Stuart's this ? '

'James Stuart, the poet-king of Scotland, who was the greatest ruler of his time.'

'Oh, but that'll never do ! What about James Second, Third, Fourth, Fifth, Sixth, Seventh—and Eighth, if you like ? No, no ! When Nature produces a great man, she doesn't make eight of the name—she doesn't make eight of the name.'

With this the red-haired man gathered his legs up on the seat, and, rolling himself into a ball, waved his newspaper in triumph and settled down to read. He glanced over every column, some, by mistake, more than once ; repeatedly his eye caught the news about Ninian Jamieson.

'Ninian Jamieson, for the fifth time!' he cried, untwisting himself, and bringing down both feet with a crash on the floor of the carriage, while he smote the newspaper between his hands as if it had been the diamond-maker's cheek.   Then he threw it to the other end of the compartment, and, arranging himself for another talk, asked of the handsome man, who watched him with a constant smile, what like Jamieson was.

'What like would you suppose him to be?' said the handsome man.

'What like?   Like a provost, of course—an eccentric provost and diamond-maker.'

'And what like's that?'

'A little man, broad, with a paunch ; hair of no particular colour, getting gray already ; a wholesale grocer, perhaps—maybe a banker.   Bemused himself when a boy with chemical tricks—read about the philosopher's stone, and the elixir of life.   Buys some platinum wire, and ammonia, and nitric acid, and a muffle-furnace, and charcoal ; hears of the Glasgow diamonds, goes mad, and makes 'em too. Is that like him?'

'Not particularly.'

'No?   He'll have a turned-up nose ; eyes small and dark ; face keen, though getting flabby ; married to a woman older than himself; six children; belongs to the Free Kirk. Eh?'

'That's not particularly like him either.'

'Well, all I can say is this,' said the little man, thoroughly disgusted, 'that my description tallies exactly with his name and quality; and if I'm not right there's something wrong, and he's not the man I took him for.'

'That's very probable.'

'But it's not probable,' said the little man, getting angry. 'Tell me the name and quality of a man, and I'll give you his physical appearance and his mental characteristics. Ninian Jamieson ought to be exactly like my description. If he's not—why, do you suppose the Fates never make mistakes? Circumstances may go all wrong, as they sometimes do. I tell you that a man's name, business, appearance and character are all interdependent; and, if he knows one, a student of human nature and history can deduce the others. Ninian Jamieson is simply a necessary exception to prove the rule. Man alive, there's the theory! Don't you see? "The surname indicates the quality; the Christian name the character." Put two and two together and you get everything else.'

The handsome man, whose smile had been broadening during the last speech of his travelling companion, burst, at its conclusion, into a great laugh.

'What!' snorted the little man, starting to his feet, 'you laugh at me!'

The tall man did not heed the remonstrance; he gave himself up to his laughter. He crowed and neighed, and went off into apoplectic gurglings and silences, only to explode again like the noise of a whole farmyard. In the climax of his fit he brought his hands down on the shoulders of the little man, and jerked out, 'You're too delightful!'

'I'm too delightful!' cried the little man, aghast. 'Too delightful! Sir!'

Words failed him; so he withdrew to the other end of the compartment, seized the paper, and began to read the leaders furiously. The storm of laughter soon subsided in the tall man, but at the first stoppage of the train the little man bundled up his traps and left the compartment, shaking the dust of it from his feet.

At three minutes past eleven, precisely three minutes late, the train stopped at Mintern. The red-haired man got out with his two portmanteaus, his umbrella, his walking-stick, and his fishing-tackle. He looked about for a porter, but he could not distinguish an olive-green suit in the throng that filled the station.

'What's the meaning of this?' he muttered. 'Where have the people come from?'

All at once a cheer burst from the crowd.

The red-haired man looked about him in a state of bewilderment. Had royalty come in the train with him? or who was this bowing gracefully as he stepped to the platform?

By heaven, it was his late companion! The

crowd surged about him. Dozens of hands shook
his. A hundred voices bellowed welcome. Quickly
a bodyguard formed, and with difficulty a way was
cloven to a carriage in attendance. There a confused
tumult arose ; the upshot being that the horses were
led away, and a dozen men harnessed instead. The
centre of a swaying mass, the carriage moved off.
Shouts and laughter filled the air, in the midst of
which the red-haired man distinguished juvenile
voices crying, ' Gie's a deemant ! '

He grew pale—one would have said his very hair
became less ruddy. He laid hold of a man, the
last of the crowd, and, detaining him by main force,
demanded who the hero was.

' The Provost,' was the answer.

' Ninian Jamieson ? '

' Yes.'

The red-haired man relaxed his grasp, and sank
down on one of his portmanteaus. ' Revenge ! ' he
muttered. ' Revenge ! '

The study of the concrete floor of a country
railway-station is neither soothing nor distracting.
The red-haired man discovered this in a few seconds,
and looking up saw a porter returning leisurely to
his duty.

' I wish my traps taken to the Mintern Arms,' he said.

'Ta 'bus is waitin',' said the porter.

Soon everything was in—he was the sole passenger—and the 'bus in motion ; but it had hardly
started when it came to a stand-still.   The cause of
the stoppage was immediately apparent.

Headed by a scratch flute-band, and surrounded
by a crowd of boys and loafers, the Provost's carriage,
drawn by the twelve volunteers, turned into the street
in front of the 'bus.   Ninian was bowing and smiling
with the bored affability of a prince.   He caught
sight of the red-haired man, and bestowed on him
a particularly gracious salute, to which the reply
was a frown.   Ninian observed the sulky expression
on the brick-dust face of the red-haired man, and
stopped his carriage.   He spoke a few words to his
human team, and a couple of stalwart poachers, confounding utterly the driver, the boots, and the red-
haired man himself, transferred the luggage to the
Provost's carriage, while a third, opening the door
of the 'bus, invited its occupant to join Mr. Jamieson
and accompany him to his residence.

The red-haired man buttoned up his little corpulent figure in his shooting-jacket, pulled his cap down
over his eyes, thrust his hands into his side pockets
with violence, straining his jacket about his waist,
and followed the Provost's messenger.   A rolling

laugh greeted him as he crossed the road, for the portentous frown he wore was very amusing. The more the crowd indulged its mirth, the fiercer grew his face, and the reciprocal action of the laughter and the frown reached a point of frenzy when the red-haired man stepped into the Provost's carriage, and flung himself down with his legs crossed defiantly and his arms tightly folded.

A brief consultation having been held by the driver and the boots, they approached the carriage with some undefined intention of re-taking their prey. The hooting of the crowd, however, and the menacing attitude of the twelve human steeds, brought them to a halt. But Ninian Jamieson, anxious to get on, prevented any dispute by throwing some silver to the hotel officials, and the procession continued its way.

Although the Provost's house was not a furlong from the station, it took a quarter of an hour to reach it, partly owing to the winding avenue which led to it, but chiefly on account of the crowd, which, accompanying the carriage to the very door, hampered its progress at every step. Arrived there, the people seemed quite satisfied with their achievement, gave three ringing cheers for their chief magistrate, and retired in good order. The twelve men who had drawn the carriage received a shilling each. They loitered about in front of the house until the last of the crowd had vanished ; then, with the help of a servant, they got away through the kitchen-garden by a back gate, and started off for Ballany, a village two miles from Mintern, where they could drink the whole of the money themselves—a consummation impossible in Mintern, as each had many drouthy friends.

The little red-haired man handed his card to the Provost the moment they entered the house.

'Mr. Cosmo Mortimer. Ha!' said the Provost, 'you are then a great man ?'

'No,' said Mortimer, 'I'm not a great man—yet. My name was Hugh Smith. Now, as it is utterly impossible for a person called Hugh Smith to attain greatness of any kind, I changed my name to Cosmo Mortimer, and I am struggling to live up to it.'

'It is a noble ambition,' said Jamieson.

'Well, it doesn't matter whether it is or not. I want to talk to you.'

'Won't you wash your hands first ? '

'No.'

'John, take these portmanteaus to the blue-room,' said Jamieson to a footman dressed in Highland garb.

'John,' said Mortimer, 'leave these portmanteaus alone.   Come, sir,'—to Jamieson—'take me where I can talk to you.'

'As you please,' said Jamieson ; and he led Mortimer into his study.

'Be seated,' said Jamieson.

'No, sir ; I'll stand.   Sir,' said Mortimer sternly, 'you owe me an apology.'

'Do I ?'

'You do.'

'I apologise, then,' said Jamieson pleasantly.

Mortimer was overwhelmed.   'How !' he cried. 'For what do you apologise ?'

'I don't know,' said Jamieson.

'Sit down, sir,' said Mortimer.   'Sit down.   I want to talk to you.'

'It was for that I brought you here.'

'For what ?'

'To have you talk to me.'

'Oh, wait till you hear what I've got to say !'

Mortimer leaned back and stretched his legs out. Resting his right heel upon his left toe, he swayed his feet from side to side, and began his speech.

'Mr. Jamieson,' he said, with a slight frown, 'the promptness of your apology has disarmed me.   Still, it is necessary that you should know for what you

have apologised.   You have apologised for six
things : first, for being called Ninian ; second, for
being called Jamieson ; third, for being Provost of
Mintern ; fourth, for being a diamond-maker ; fifth,
for laughing at me ; sixth, for not telling me at
once in the train that you were Ninian Jamieson,
Provost of Mintern, and diamond-maker.   Now, do
you adhere to your apology ? '

'I do,' said Jamieson.   'I apologise for each and
all of these things.'

Mortimer was dissatisfied.   An apology to be
thoroughly enjoyed must be drawn like a tooth.   It
must be forthcoming only to invincible argument, or
the dread of a horsewhip.   To fling an apology in
one's face is to repeat the insult in an intensified
form.   Mortimer knew that he himself would not
apologise in such an off-hand way as Jamieson had
done except to some one whom he regarded as of
no account.   He dreaded nothing more than sleeve-
laughter, and he thought he heard the little fiend
chuckling at Jamieson's right cuff.   He was endeavouring to hit on some subtle expression which might
open up the whole question again without seeming
to do so, in order to test Jamieson's sincerity, when
the latter laid before him a new aspect of the matter.

'And now,' he said, 'suppose you apologise to me.'

'What !' cried Mortimer, springing to his feet.

'There's no need for these explosions,' said Jamieson. 'I want you to talk to me, not to bellow at me. Sit down. Yes,' continued Jamieson ; 'it has occurred to me that you might wish to express regret for having slandered a man whom you knew nothing about.'

'To what do you refer?' asked Mortimer judicially.

'I refer,' said Jamieson, with his bland smile, 'to your detraction of myself.'

'I deny the detraction.'

Mortimer leaned back in his chair, built up his feet again, and prepared to discuss.

'Explain yourself,' said Jamieson.

'I said you were eccentric : you are. I alleged that Jamieson was a provostal name : I repeat the allegation. I asserted that you weren't a great man : I reassert it. I insisted that a diamond-maker couldn't be a great man, and I stand to it. I described your appearance wrongly, but on your assuring me of that I immediately withdrew my description. I summed up by explaining to you that you were a freak of Nature, or one of Fate's mistakes—possibly a mixture of both ; and I will defend these positions with my last breath.'

'That's very good,' said Jamieson, laughing.

Mortimer was more dissatisfied than ever. He felt convinced that Jamieson was not taking him seriously. He had been slow to admit it, although the idea had been present from the beginning of his intercourse with the Provost. Now he determined to bring it to an issue.

'What do you think of me?' he asked bluntly.

Jamieson looked at him for half a minute and then said, 'I think you'll do very well.'

'Do!—do what?'

'I'll tell you after lunch.'

'But I'll not stay to lunch,' said Mortimer stoutly. 'You're a bully, sir, I see, as well as an eccentric, and you're a young man, and you seem to be accustomed to have your way here. Doubtless you're cock of the walk in Mintern, but you'll not crow over me.'

The Provost rose and put his back against the door.

'Have you business in Mintern?' he asked.

'Business!' cried Mortimer. 'Sir, I'm a gentleman.'

'Then you're here on pleasure?'

'No, sir. I'm here to fish.'

'As a duty?' queried the Provost.

'No ; as sport,' said Mortimer.   'Sport, pleasure,
duty, are three distinct things.'

'Then you'll stay with me as long as you are
in Mintern,' said the Provost.   At the same time
he took down a huge broadsword that hung beside
the door, and flourished it about Mortimer's head.
Mortimer winked and drew in his breath, but said
nothing.

'John,' said the Provost, opening the door,
'take Mr. Mortimer's portmanteaus to the blue-
room.'

CHAPTER II

THE 'DUNMYATT WHISKY'

LUNCH was served in a hall containing a long table, at the head of which was a dais. Here Jamieson and Mortimer sat, while the servants, having set the dishes, took their places beneath the salt. Before each was a good-sized wooden bowl or cog, containing porridge, a smaller cog with milk, and a horn spoon of very unfashionable dimensions. As soon as Jamieson had taken a first spoonful all the servants began to sup without ceremony. Mortimer, who had no particular relish for porridge, devoured cogs and spoons, master and servants, with his eyes.

'Fa' tae, man,' said Jamieson.

'What?' cried Mortimer.

He knew the Scotch dialect well enough, but was so unprepared for it that, although he heard the words distinctly, he had no sense of their meaning.

'Don't you like porridge?' asked Jamieson.

Mortimer determined that a warier conduct than his had been for the last hour or two might be advisable. The hall in which they were had quite the appearance of an armoury, with targets and claymores, blunderbusses and pistols, on all the walls. He was beginning also to doubt the sanity of his entertainer. So, while he would have preferred to propound a theory regarding porridge which occurred to him at the moment, he said, in answer to the Provost's question, 'I like it very much indeed, but I am so astonished at all I see that I'm afraid I've lost my appetite.'

'Try it,' said the Provost. 'We're noted for our porridge here.'

Mortimer took one spoonful, and then another. 'It's the best porridge I ever tasted,' he said with genuine satisfaction. 'It's very different,' he added tautologically, 'from any porridge I've been accustomed to.'

'You mean the thick, raw, half-boiled stuff which is thought to be the true Scotch dish?'

'But is it not?' said Mortimer.

'Well, I hardly know. I'm sorry if it is, for I can't take it. This is boiled for fully half an hour with, as you see, lots of water. Isn't it, cook?'

'Yes, sir,' answered a magnificent female, immediately below the salt.

This concluded the conversation for the time. Mortimer's spoon was as busy as those of the others, and every cog stood empty almost at the same instant. The wooden dishes were then removed, and drinking horns with silver rims set in their places. A pretty maid-servant took from an aumry a large stone jug and a formidable glass. Having curtsied to the Provost, who promptly rose and kissed her, she filled the glass and poured it into her master's horn. She seemed in doubt what to do next, but Jamieson nodded towards Mortimer, and she advanced and curtsied to him. He thrust his chair from the table, placed his hands on his knees with the backs of them downward, squaring his elbows, and stared the girl out of countenance.

'Everything here,' said the Provost, who was not quite well pleased, 'is as innocent and wholesome as the porridge.'

'I know, I know!' cried Mortimer. 'I'm only admiring.'

He rose with awkward ceremony. His face had resolved into such a ludicrous expression of beatification that the girl blushed and smothered a laugh as he kissed her. Then she filled a glass into his

horn, and set the jug at the cook's right hand.   The
cook took half a glass and passed the jug to the
coachman, who dealt himself full measure, and so it

went round the servants, the maids and a boy in
buttons taking a half, and the men a whole glass.
The Provost drank first, and after him all the
servants.   Mortimer thought by the bouquet and

the dark colour that the beverage was whisky which
had been kept in sherry-wood.   He liked whisky
well enough, but he had always regarded the drinking of neat spirits as a habit vulgar and depraved ;
and, forgetting his late resolution, was about to
attack the custom in his most dogmatic and diffuse
manner when Jamieson said, 'Drink it, man.   It's
a hundred years old.'

'Might I not have a little water?' suggested
Mortimer.

'A single drop of water spoils it.   Doesn't it,
cook?' said the Provost.

'It does indeed, sir,' answered the cook deferen-
tially, but with undeniable enthusiasm.

Seeing no help for it, Mortimer put the horn to
his mouth and drank it off.   The effect was in-
stantaneous.

'By Jove!' he cried, 'that's very fine.   As you
say, a single drop of water would altogether dis-
organise this whisky.   I perceive five flavours in it.
First of all there is the flavour of maturity ; secondly,
there still remains a perceptible, a barely perceptible
breath of the peat-reek ; thirdly, there is a subdued dash of the wood in which it has been kept ;
fourthly, a distinct aroma of the sherry which
preceded it in the wood ; fifthly, and lastly, and

probably principally, I carried to the horn the sweet freshness of your maid-servant's rosy cheek. Sir, this whisky has a creamy consistence, a mellowness as of ripe fruit—and yet there is a grasp in it, an appeal, a penetrating virtuosity, a pervasive subtlety, that defies further definition.’

‘You've made mistakes,’ said Jamieson. ‘There's no flavour of sherry, but there's something else.’

‘Let me see,’ said Mortimer. ‘Ah! I think I know. Stolen sweets?’

‘Right,’ replied Jamieson. ‘It has the air of the Ochils about it, and never paid duty.’

‘I was certain there was something escaping me,’ said Mortimer. ‘I felt it while I was defining. Doubtless the full definition would have occurred to me without your suggestion after another glass of the whisky.’

‘Doubtless,’ said the Provost, rising.

Mortimer and the servants immediately followed his example. The latter left the room one by one in order of precedence, the maids first, beginning with the cook, and they all bowed or curtsied at the door as they withdrew.

‘Mary,’ said the Provost, addressing the maid who had served the whisky, ‘take the jug and two horns to the study.’

'Sir,' said Mortimer, when they had returned to
the Provost's sanctum, 'half an hour ago you promised to tell me in this room what you think of me.
Before you do so I should like to hear the history of
this liquor. For the moment it interests me more
than my own personality.'

'Certainly; because I cannot tell you the one
without the other.'

'That is very remarkable,' said Mortimer. 'There
can be no doubt that you are eccentric. Elements
of greatness there may be, but eccentric you are in
the highest degree. Could you give me a short
sketch of your life? I am no idle gossip, but deeply
in earnest. I search for the theory that underlies
the phenomena of existence.'

'In order to give you the history of this whisky,
in order to give you my opinion of yourself, it is
necessary that you should have a short account of
my life.'

'I thank heaven that I have met you, sir,' said
Mortimer. 'You are like a skeleton-clock: theory
is visible through every transparent circumstance of
your life, and every circumstance of your life seems
to be transparent.'

'You shall judge,' said Jamieson. 'My father
kept a shop in Mintern. He was a grocer.'

'Ha! you are a grocer's son, then!' cried
Mortimer.

'Quite so; a licensed grocer's son. He had a
respectable business, and lived comfortably. I was
his only child, and got so much of my own way that
by the age of ten I governed my parents absolutely.
I had two passions common to boys—novel-reading
and exploring. Look here!'

The Provost showed Mortimer a room opening
off the study. Mortimer entered it, and found the
walls shelved from floor to ceiling, and each shelf
packed with books. When they resumed their seats
Jamieson sat musing for a minute or two, and
Mortimer looked about the room, observing it more
carefully than he had yet done. Deerskins almost
covered the floor; an oaken writing-table occupied
the window recess; the ceiling was of oak; old oak
chairs, and new ones in imitation of the old, stood
against the walls, which were covered with long-
bows, cross-bows, halberts, Andrea Ferraras, claymores, targets, horse-pistols, and some old pictures.
Two suits of armour stood in corners. There were
only a few books; these were bound in calf, and
stood on two carved oak shelves beside the carved
oak mantelpiece. They were all Scotch, and
included *The Tales of a Grandfather*, Drummond's

Five Jameses, and Bellenden's Translation of Boece.

'There are two thousand novels in that room,' said Jamieson, rousing himself from his brown study, and interrupting Mortimer's inventory, 'all which I had read before I was eighteen. At that age I stopped novels, and haven't opened one since. So much for one passion. The other continues un-abated ; and I have been all over Europe, not in trains, but on my feet, or on horseback. At the age of ten, of course, my explorations were confined to the neighbourhood of Mintern. Within a radius of twenty miles I knew every village, every ruin, every glen, every loch, and had climbed all the highest hills. From Benchonzie to Dunmyatt, from Moredun Top to Ben Ledi I rambled at will. In the summer I was often away from home for days together, sometimes sleeping in a haystack ; but as a rule I had money to pay for a bed. At the outset of my travels I preferred the Ochils to the Grampians, and delighted especially to climb Dunmyatt. One morning shortly after I had turned my twelfth year——'

'I beg you to observe, Mr. Jamieson,' said Mortimer, who thought he noticed a gradual assumption of distinction in the style of the narrative, and in the attitude of the narrator, 'that all this points only to eccentricity ; not by any means to greatness.'

'Be that as it may,' said Jamieson, with his bland smile, 'on this particular morning a great desire to get to the top of Dunmyatt overtook me on my way to school. I threw my books over a wall and set off. Had I gone home I could easily have persuaded my parents to let me have a holiday, but, however certain of victory, I always hated argument, and avoided it in those days, and for years after, no matter at what cost to others. The distance from Mintern to the western end of the Ochils is twelve miles, so that it was one o'clock before I arrived at a farm at the foot of Dunmyatt where I was known. I got dinner there, and in an hour after, the ascent being very easy, I was on the top of the hill. I had, of course, a novel with me—I never went anywhere at that time, school, bed, or church, without one— and read it through before I thought of descending. I went down the south side of the hill, intending to go to Blairlogie, a small village at the foot of Dunmyatt. I knew an old woman there with whom I meant to take tea. On the way I turned aside to have another look at an old copper-mine, which I had examined repeatedly, always in the hope of finding an entrance and a hidden treasure. This

D

time I determined to make a thorough search. I attacked with vigour a considerable excavation—one of several dug by myself on former visits—making use of a rusty shovel left there doubtless by some previous explorer. I worked at such a rate that in five minutes I was out of breath, and had to rest. Leaning on the shovel I looked up the hillside, and saw the entrance to a small cave which I had often examined, but had never thought of connecting with the mine. That idea occurred to me forcibly there and then, and I went up, shovel in hand. When I had dug about a foot into the floor of the cave I struck wood. Excitement increased my strength, and in a little while I had uncovered a lid about four feet square. One side of it rested on what proved to be a wooden slide into the mine ; the other three sides rested on the rock. On lifting off the lid my heart gave a great bound. I saw a round hole three feet in diameter, and the top of an inclined plane—the way I had no doubt to fabulous adventures. With scarcely a moment's hesitation I stepped in, and lying face downwards on the slide, which was two and a half feet broad, I clutched the sides of it and began to descend. I found the slope so gentle, however, that progress in that way was not only laborious but unnecessary. I therefore got

to my feet, and going back to the entrance took my
shovel.   Pressing it in my right hand against the
side of the plane to guide me, I walked boldly down,
counting my steps after the approved fashion in such
adventures : thirty of my steps ended the descent.
My eyes had already accustomed themselves to the
semi-darkness, and I beheld an array of little barrels
which I at once concluded would be full of jewels
and ancient, or at least, foreign, gold and silver
coins, with a little bullion.   I searched about hoping
to find an old hammer, or something with which to
break open one of the barrels, but as the mine had
not been worked for a great many years there were
few traces of its origin, and nothing at all in the
shape of a hammer.   I was forced to use the shovel,
my knife, and at last my foot.   The shovel broke,
the blade of my knife snapped off, and in despair I
brought my heel down on the bung of the barrel I
had attacked.   Once, twice, and the third time it
gave way, and I was splashed with whisky !   I cried
with disgust and vexation.   All the barrels were of
the same pattern; and I judged, correctly, of the
same contents.   My first adventure, which a few
minutes before had promised to my imagination a
whole Arabia of wonder, to end in a few whisky-
barrels !   I rushed up the slide, striking my head

rather severely against the rock as I approached the
exit, and, without making any attempt to conceal
what I had done, went down to Blairlogie. The old
woman gave me tea, after which I lay down on the
sofa in her parlour and slept till daybreak. I ate
some bread and left the house without wakening my
hostess. Being now quite good-humoured about my
adventure, I climbed to the cave, and going into the
mine, counted the barrels : there were fifty of them.
I then covered the entrance with care and walked
over the hill to Mintern, where I arrived shortly
before breakfast. My father wouldn't at first believe
my story, but I was so positive that he went to
Dunmyatt with me next day. On the road home,
the truth of my discovery having been established,
my father was very meditative. About half-way he
asked me if I had told anybody except himself.
This I had not done ; and I remember distinctly,
having assured my father that he was my only con-
fidant, with what curiosity I watched his face for the
rest of the way. A melancholy smile played over
it. Beginning in a slight frown, it stole into his
eyes, expanded his nostrils, and went out in a twitching of his upper lip. He had the reputation of
being eccentric——'

'What was his first name ?'

The Provost started, for he had forgotten Mortimer's presence, and a smile like that he had described flitted across his face.

'William James,' he answered.

'William James Jamieson!' cried Mortimer. 'Eccentric! I should think so! William James, Jean Jacques, Jean Paul! You see, double Christian names of that kind always denote eccentricity.'

'Your theory seems to have some foundation,' said Jamieson, and was about to continue his narrative, but Mortimer had caught fire.

'Some foundation!' he cried. 'Its basis is the law of heredity. No one except an eccentric person will give an eccentric name. Some foundation! Why, you find it everywhere! Ay, even in the Bible; although I believe most exceptions are to be found among Biblical names, especially in antediluvian times. Still, look at Methuselah! Do you think he wasn't eccentric? Do you think a man who lived for nine hundred and sixty-nine years wasn't eccentric? Do you think his father wasn't eccentric? Why, Enoch was one of the most eccentric men who ever lived, because he was one of the best, and he didn't die. Look at Adam! Do you think he wasn't eccentric? and Eve too?

Man, they must have been eccentric. Do you
know, I'm beginning to think that everybody and
every name is eccentric. Because, don't you see, if
the names which are eccentric at present were common, then the common names would be eccentric.
That, however, would do away with greatness altogether.'

'No doubt,' said Jamieson, laughing. 'But you
must let me get on with my story.'

'What are you laughing at?' cried Mortimer.
'Do you think I'm a fool?'

'Have patience,' said Jamieson, 'I'm coming to
that. But you will require to hear the whole history of my life before you will be in a position to
know what I think of you.——My father had formed
a plan on the way home from Dunmyatt. He took
a house at once in Blairlogie, and we went there for
the summer. He drove to Mintern every morning,
carrying with him sometimes one, sometimes two of
the barrels; and in less than two months he had
transferred them all, not to his shop, but to this
house, which he had recently bought, and which was
then only a third of its present size. He sent
samples of the whisky to analysts and doctors, and
the gentry in the neighbourhood; got it noticed in
the *Lancet*, and advertised it widely. It soon had a

great sale, and he made lots of money. I was
twelve when I found the barrels, and my father died
when I was twenty-six. During these fourteen
years the "Dunmyatt Whisky" was sold by the
hogshead every day. Once or twice I wondered
how my father kept up the supply, but it didn't
concern me much, and I never asked him. He in-
vested his money as he made it, and he was always
lucky. My mother and he died within a few weeks
of each other, and I was left with £150,000. On
his death-bed my father said very little, and passed
away with a smile exactly like that which had interested me fourteen years before on the way home
from Dunmyatt: a scarcely perceptible contraction
of the brows; a faint gleam in the eye, half comic,
half pathetic; and a slight curl of the lip which
death undid the moment it appeared.'

Here Jamieson paused, staring at the toes of his
boots, and Mortimer felt constrained to cough and
to replenish his glass.

'Mr. Jamieson,' said Mortimer, wiping his mouth
and flecking his eyes with his handkerchief, 'let me
congratulate you on this distinct exhibition of greatness. It may be in a small matter—most people
have to lose their fathers—but an inferior man
would have flaunted his sorrow with a " He was a

good father to me ; I wish I had been a better son,"
or something of that kind, fishing for the approbation
of his auditor.   Now, you———'

'Be quiet!' cried Jamieson, flashing out in a tone
and a look which astonished Mortimer.   'Keep your
dilettantism for suitable subjects.'

Mortimer gulped his whisky in alarm ; but Jamieson had resumed the contemplation of his boots.
Two minutes of great uneasiness followed this out-
burst, and then the Provost looked up with his bland
smile.   He said nothing, however, and Mortimer
broke the silence.

'Did you ever find,' he asked, 'how your father
kept the whisky going?'

'I shall tell you what I found,' said Jamieson.
'I found a key in my father's desk with this written
on the label—

> '"In a cellar numbered two
>   You'll find the source of all my wealth.
> I am dead but, Ninian, you
>   Still may drink my soul's good health."

In the cellar I found forty barrels of the " Dunmyatt
Whisky " unbroached.'

'Where had he got them?'

'They were the original barrels intact.   He had
used ten of them in preparing samples, and kept the

other forty. What he sold was a judicious blend of quite modern distillation.'

'How very like William James Jamieson!' exclaimed Mortimer.

'Once a week we have a porridge lunch with a taste of the whisky. We never drink it on any other occasion except on my father's birthday, as I wish to make it last as long as possible.'

'Mr. Jamieson, have you ever reposed this confidence in another?'

'No, you are the first man I've told.'

'Then,' said Mr. Mortimer complacently, 'I can in some measure gather what your opinion of me is.'

But the Provost only smiled like his father.

'And I may also conclude something from the fact that you have departed in my favour from your custom as regards the "Dunmyatt Whisky,"' said Mortimer, helping himself again.

This remark also elicited only a smile.

'Do you know anything of the history of this whisky prior to your finding it?' asked Mortimer.

'Nothing whatever,' said Jamieson. 'My father, I believe, made indirect inquiries, but without result. You can understand how he couldn't investigate the matter thoroughly.'

'Quite,' said Mortimer. 'But have you done nothing?'

'Nothing; it doesn't interest me in the least.'

'By the bye, what led you to become Provost of Mintern?'

'That's very simple. Some months after the death of my father, the provostship falling vacant, I was asked to join the council in order to be elected to that office. The good people were so dazzled with the fortune my father had left that they would, I believe, have made me absolute monarch of the world had it rested with them.'

'And what made you stop reading novels?' asked Mortimer.

'That's just the point where I intend to resume my story,' said Jamieson. 'I gave up novels because I had begun to read history—Scotch history. It was Scott's *Tales of a Grandfather* that started me; but I soon had a very particular reason for continuing the study. You must know that when the Chevalier de St. George, otherwise James III of England and VIII of Scotland, was in this country in 1715 he married privately Marjory Morton, the daughter of the Laird of Tullibolton. Shortly after James left this country his wife died in giving birth to a son. Sheriffmuir had destroyed the

Jacobite hopes of Morton of Tullibolton, and he
became a staunch supporter of the Guelf dynasty.
He called his grandson James Jamieson, and gave
him to a farmer to rear.   When the boy grew up
he received a farm on the estate of Tullibolton, and
was generally considered an illegitimate son of the
laird's.   He didn't care for farming, however, and
joined a foot regiment ; and it is said that he fought
against his step-brother, Prince Charles Edward, at
Culloden.'

'Sir,' said Mortimer, 'I have read a little Scotch
history, but I don't remember a word of all
this.'

'There is no printed record of it,' said Jamieson,
'but I have documents to prove its truth, and you
shall see them. Let me finish the story first. James
Jamieson returned to Tullibolton in his fortieth
year, and married a ploughman's daughter.   Morton
had been dead for some time, but he had left
Jamieson a farm, which he had bought for that
purpose, his estate being entailed.   In the beginning
of this century James Jamieson's great-great-grand-
son, my great-grandfather, sold the farm and removed
to Mintern, where he began the business which my
father inherited.   Perhaps, since you have some
acquaintance with Scotch history, you may remember

that the so-called direct line of the Stuart race terminated in the Cardinal Frascati, who called himself Henry IX. By his death in 1807 the true direct line was left without a rival ; and as I am the sole representative of that branch, I am legitimately, and by divine right, Ninian I., King of Great Britain, France, and Ireland.'

Mortimer sat up in his chair and stared at the Provost. He was now convinced of his insanity ; and Jamieson's serenity, after making such an astounding announcement, was, in Mortimer's mind, confirmation enough of the fact, had it needed any.

'You will now understand,' continued the Provost, assuming unconsciously a lordlier tone, 'the nature of my interest in Scotch history.. It was an exceedingly opportune event in my life, the discovery at the age of eighteen of my rank and title ; for, as the result of my novel reading, I was the prey of a morbid ambition. I burned with a desire to distinguish myself in some heroic but unheard-of way. What appeared to me the utter paltriness of all possible careers, combined with my failure to conceive of one hitherto impossible, but which would open a path to my genius, drove me mad for a short time. My father had with reluctance determined to remove me to an asylum, when I suddenly regained my sanity. It was the accidental discovery of the facts which I have briefly narrated to you that brought back my scattered senses.'

'How did you make the discovery?' asked Mortimer.

'I do not intend to enter on that just now,' said Jamieson. 'On some future occasion I may perhaps satisfy your curiosity. That the facts are true you need have no doubt: I give you my word. Some-time I will show you the documents. For more than a year the mere knowledge of who I was satisfied my ambition, and the study of the lives of my ancestors occupied my time. Then I gave myself up to dreams of sovereignty, leaping over entirely the period of struggle. The mental strain of this continuous dream—for it was with me day and night—produced a time of extreme lassitude, during which I made my first tour on the continent. After my return the dream was in abeyance for more than a year, but it seized me again with a shock like the recollection of an unfulfilled duty; such, indeed, it had become to me. I shirked it, however, and went back to the continent, where I managed to smother my aspirations—my true self—for a time; but only for a time. I remember it was in Bucharest that

my destiny again laid hold of me. I had been
gambling a little. Tired of the sordid excitement
I went up to the top of the house. The sun was
sinking in the plain, and its last rays shed a lustre
over the many-coloured roofs of the broad city,
embowered in its gardens. The towers and domes
of its hundred churches glowed and flashed like
inlaid blades and shields. The narrow tortuous
streets wound like serpents, bright with the hues of
the robes and rags of the crowds that filled them.
It was fair-time at Giurgevo, the port of Bucharest,
and hundreds of people from every nation in Asia
mingled with the inhabitants. Whether it was the
spires and domes that recalled to me our targets
and claymores, or the rainbow-coloured crowds that
reminded me of the tartans, I was not sufficiently
self-conscious at the time to observe, but there leapt
out on the sky a vision of the battle of Culloden.
The shrieks, shouts, laughter, and outlandish music
ascending from the streets mingled with the vision.
I watched it long, and it vanished only when I began
unwittingly to recite Aytoun's ballad—

' " Chief and vassal, lord and yeoman, there they lie in heaps
        together,
    Smitten by the deadly volley, rolled in blood upon the
        heather ;

And the Hanoverian horsemen, fiercely riding to and
    fro,
Deal their murderous strokes at random. . . . Woe is
    me! where am I now?"

'I had no sleep that night, and next morning I
started for Scotland. All the way home scheme
after scheme chased each other through my head.
At one time I determined to enter Parliament and
proceed in a constitutional manner. It seemed to
me a very simple thing to form a party, principally
in the House of Lords, and to mature it for my reign.
"The lords," I said to myself, "are not nearly alive
to the splendid position in which they now are. One
or two of them seem to have grasped it, but they
wish to keep it to themselves in order that they may
lead. Nothing can ever be done in that way. The
whole body of the aristocracy must lead the nation;
they must not allow themselves tamely to be swamped
by capital. Their reply to those who want to tamper
with land must be a demand for the redistribution of
capital. Let them go to the people with that, and
there will be no more tinkering at the Upper Chamber
for a hundred years to come." You see I thoroughly
understood the true method of constitutional government: to pit class against class in the bitterest feud.
It's as old as Caius Gracchus, and older. Well,

having organised a strong party among the lords,
I should have waited until I became prime minister ;
then, heading a revolution prepared by myself, I
should have seized the crown. Another plan was to
enter the army and, having obtained a position of
power, to rebel, but this did not seem so certain a
way as the other. Sometimes I thought to further
my design chiefly through the press, by starting a
Jacobite newspaper or magazine. There was besides
a very simple plan which commended itself to me
for a brief space : to state to Britain in a modest
address who I was, and that I had abandoned the
legend of my family and was quite prepared to
govern exactly as the nation required. By the time
I got home my excitement had produced brain-fever,
and when I recovered, although thoroughly conscious
of who I was, a whole year of contentment followed.
Then I began to read Carlyle, and I have had no
rest since the day I opened *Heroes and Hero-worship*.
I feel in myself the power to govern Britain as it has
never been governed. I have the strength, if I can
wrench from fate the opportunity, to weld together
the English-speaking nations ; to make New York
the capital of a Britain greater than Dilke's ; to
shake the Russian empire to pieces, like an ill-made
garment, the work of sweaters ; to plant the cross in

Constantinople; to people Africa; to open China; to dictate to the world. I fought with myself; I tried to learn Greek; I tried to paint; I read biographies in the hope of being attracted by some other career than that of a claimant to the throne of Britain. The life of Benvenuto Cellini charmed me, and I began to work in metals. Here is the sole result.'

Jamieson opened a drawer in his writing-table and handed Mortimer a small leather case. Mortimer took from it a roughly-made medal, on the face of which was a likeness of the Provost with the words 'NINIANUS PRIMUS, BRITANNIAE REX, F. D.'; and on the reverse, the royal arms with 'GRATIA DEI, SED NON VOLUNTATE HOMINUM.'

Said Mortimer, who had recovered from his astonishment, and was in his most critical mood, 'Did you make this while your father was alive?'

'Yes,' said Jamieson.

'Then you were only Prince of Wales at that time.'

'True,' said Jamieson; 'but I tested my father often in many indirect ways, and found that he knew nothing of his rank. Of course, had I achieved my object in his lifetime, I would have made him king. Well, when I was elected Provost the old idea of entering Parliament returned, so I set about making

E

myself popular, an object I attained.   I have also
managed to keep the people at a distance, chiefly by
never appearing in the streets except in my carriage.'

'Admirable!' burst out Mortimer.   'I see theory
there.   But go on.'

'The news of the making of diamonds in Glasgow
modified my plans.   Fifty diamonds worth £100,000
each would be £5,000,000.   With such a capital one
might become anything.   I fitted up a laboratory,
and after working for two years succeeded yesterday
in producing two diamonds.'

Jamieson took from his vest-pocket a pill-box
and handed it to Mortimer.

'In my excitement,' continued the Provost, 'I
told the correspondent of the *Scotsman*, and he com-
municated the news to his paper.   But at night I
submitted one of the diamonds to a greater pressure
than I had at first employed, and it was crushed to a
paste ; you see it there in the box.   The other one
looks all right, but it is soft at the core.   You can
imagine how chagrined I was.   The last train had
left hours before I made the hideous discovery.   I
hired a cab and four horses and drove to Edinburgh,
but I was too late to prevent the appearance of my
over-hasty communication.'

Why didn't you telegraph ?'

'I couldn't; it would have been known far and wide in Mintern next day. The reporter I bribed, but I couldn't bribe the postmaster, and he is one of my principal enemies in the town, and the telegram at that time of night could not have been despatched without his cognisance. On my road to the train this morning I resolved to beat no more about the bush, but to throw everything else aside and make a dash for the crown. I forgot my chagrin the moment my resolution was taken; and the reception I had at the station showed me the necessity of leaving Mintern at once. I understand popularity sufficiently to know that when the people learn that they have been, as they will say, "hoaxed," no explanation will satisfy them, and they will despise me because of their own absurd conduct of to-day. My chance of the membership is gone; besides, I tell you frankly, I couldn't stand the nods and winks and grins that would meet me everywhere.'

'But why not go on with your diamonds, and make them as hard-hearted as they need to be?'

'I don't think it's possible; and I couldn't repeat the process, for it was as much chance as good guiding that produced these miserable spongy sparks. And then I'm tired of waiting and dreaming. I must act.'

The Provost rose, and marched up and down the room with long strides, erect head, and flaming eyes.

'And now,' said Mortimer, 'what has all this got to do with your opinion of me?'

'Ah!' replied the Provost, resuming his seat, 'I had forgotten that. When you came into the train with your funny little fat body, and short squint legs, and your staring red hair, and round goggle eyes, looking as important as all the Mintern town-councillors rolled into one, something whispered to me that we would be better acquainted; and when you began to talk I saw at once how it was to be. You must know that when I am king I intend to revive many of the customs of the feudal monarchs; and it occurred to me to start at once by appointing you my court-jester, my fool. Yes,' continued the Provost, unabashed by the pallor of Mortimer's face and the ruddy glare of his eyes, 'all your speech and action, and the droll reason for changing your name, mark you out as well fitted for a professional fool. You little dreamt, I expect, when you were cultivating your ridiculous gestures, and developing your grotesque style of speech—and it must have cost you some trouble— that you were obeying that transcendent law which is called Chance. You with your ardent desire to

amuse your fellowmen, unappreciated hitherto, meet
me who have a kingly desire to be amused in my
moments of leisure by just that titillation of the
intellect which it is the aim of your life to produce.
You at once begin your fooling in your best form
without any introduction, and I at once appreciate
you at your full value. Chance may be the only term
for such meetings as ours, but let us understand
by Chance an occult phase of Destiny. I may tell
you that I admire you very much indeed.'

Mortimer was on his legs. His very hair had
turned pale ; his eyes were blood-shot, and a slight
foam oozed from his lips. He struck an heroic
attitude, his right foot advanced and his left hand
clenched at his side. With the forefinger of his
right hand rigidly extended he made violent stabs
at the Provost.

'I have an annuity,' he cried, 'an annuity of
£400. I am a man of education—of culture. I
have not read two thousand novels, nor addled my
brains with Scotch history ; but I have all the
common sense I was born with. I'm not six feet,
and straight, and black-eyed, but I have a sanguine
complexion, and I can tell you it is a complexion
much more capable of greatness than your passionate
bilious hue that burns to ashes in license and mad-

ness. I play the fool! I have brains, sir, more brains than body. You have body, sir, more body than brains; and I am king, and you are fool, by all the laws—by all the laws! It was exactly men of your calibre that sank to court-jesters long ago—men with more body and blood than brains and sense. Your imagination has broken the halter; you can't be shod, sir; you are incapable of any serious undertaking, of any abstruse thinking. I play a part! I be anything else than myself! I tell you I have an annuity of £400, and a house in Edinburgh; and I am forty and a bachelor. And I do what I like, and I say what I like, and I go where I like; and I'm going now, sir. I want to hear no more of your brain-sick humbug—your porridge, and your watered whisky, and your kings, and your ninnies, and your *Ninianus*. Ha, ha, ha! *Ninianus primus*—the prize ninny! Ha, ha, ha!'

'That's only passable, Cosmo,' said the Provost, 'only passable. You have strained yourself and overdone it; your assumed sincerity almost became real. But you must be tired, Cosmo; you have done some very good fooling—quite sufficient for one day. Don't make any effort. You have shown most indubitable ability as a clown, and you may rest on your oars, Cosmo. I'm going to call you

Cosmo. It suits your profession admirably. Triboulet, Chicot, Scogan, Bonny—Cosmo; your name is quite fit to come at the tail of these, and I believe you will make as good and loyal a fool as any of them. And so, Cosmo, I have let you know all about myself, because the great kings took their fools into their confidence, and I will ask your advice sometimes, as they did.'

Mortimer, who after his passionate speech had sunk down exhausted, sprang to his feet again more enraged than before.

'You misunderstand me wilfully,' he cried. 'You are a miserable *farceur*, and I despise you. I have written for newspapers, and I'll put you into a sketch with all your follies—by name, sir, by name; and you can summon me for libel and welcome. I'll *libel* you! I'll make you worse than you are; I'll make you the laughing-stock of Scotland—by name, sir, by name. And I shall leave your hideous inaesthetic house at once, sir; and I shall expose *it* too, sir.'

'Cosmo, Cosmo, take care,' said Jamieson, as one would address a dog, intercepting Mortimer, who moved toward the door.

'I shall be bullied no longer,' screamed Mortimer. Boiling with anger and whisky he snatched a claymore from the wall and brandished it with unscientific

vigour. 'Make way there !' he cried, imitating to
the best of his ability some position which he had
seen on the stage.

Jamieson, with his back to the door, took down
the immense weapon which had already helped
Mortimer to make up his mind, and put himself
with almost as much awkwardness as his opponent
into an attitude of defence.   The heavy broadsword
was quite pliable in Jamieson's hands; but Mortimer,
observing that he had no better idea of fencing than
himself, thought he saw his advantage.   He lowered
his claymore, retired a few steps, and, although he
had difficulty in restraining himself, succeeded in
addressing the Provost with the gravity of a champion
about to engage in mortal combat.

'I perceive,' he said, 'that you know nothing at
all about *l'escrime*.   Now, when I was in Paris, I went
two or three times a week to the Bois de Boulogne,
and was invariably victorious.   I have a cut which
is simply irresistible, thus,' and Mortimer placed himself in an agonising position, which he maintained with
difficulty for the space of three seconds, and went
through an involute series of curves and thrusts as if
he had been describing a lover's knot in the air.   Recovering himself just in time to escape a fall he stuck
the point of his sword in a deer-skin, and resting his

left hand on his hip examined the effect of his per-
formance on the Provost. It was satisfactory, he
thought ; but he mistook what was merely vexation
for anxiety. The Provost was cursing that restless indolence of his which had led him to dream
so much and wander so far, but had left him wholly
unacquainted with a necessary kingly accomplish-
ment. Mortimer imagined he was thinking out
some dignified method of withdrawing from the
quarrel.

'So,' resumed the professed duellist, 'you had
better not insist on what can only end in bloodshed.
Let me go quietly, and——'

'Come, Cosmo,' the Provost interrupted, understanding that Mortimer lied, 'let us try this deadly
cut.'

With that he advanced from the door, holding
the pommel of his broadsword against his breast,
the blade projecting six feet in front of him.
Mortimer made repeated slashes at it, but failed to
do more than sway it a little as Jamieson grasped
the hilt with both hands ; and when Mortimer tried
a flank movement the Provost wheeled his point into
position. Soon the little man was pinned against
the wall.

'Now or never is the time for the cut,' said

Jamieson, pressing the point in a button-hole of Mortimer's vest.

'Don't,' said Mortimer pathetically, dropping his sword.

The Provost immediately released him, and Mortimer hung the claymore on the wall and went back to his chair.

'I'm a coward,' he groaned. 'I'm not a great man. I'm only Hugh Smith. Cosmo Mortimer would have died against that wall.'

The Provost hung up his weapon also, and was about to resume his seat when a gong sounded.

'Half-past five,' he said. 'We've had a long talk. Dinner's at six. Come and dress.'

CHAPTER III

THE Provost's dressing-room was immediately above the study, and as large as it. A little room opened off it, corresponding to that which contained the novels below; it was his bedroom. Two entire sides of the dressing-room were fitted up as a wardrobe, one with shelves three feet broad, and the other with pegs; sliding panels of oak extended from floor to ceiling; and as the other walls were wainscotted in oak, the existence of the wardrobe could not easily be detected. In the centre of this apartment mirrors were arranged as in a tailor's fitting-on room. The rest of the furnishings were not distinguished by any peculiarity.

'Now,' said the Provost, 'I have a great many costumes here. There are the princely fashions of half a dozen centuries for myself, and a variety of garbs in which I sometimes dress my servants; among them is the very thing for you.'

The Provost moved a panel and took from the wardrobe a cap with ass's ears and a cock's comb, having a bell on each ear and on the comb; a coat, the skirt of which was cut into peaks, with immense peaks at the elbows; and a pair of tights. One half of each of these garments was red, the other yellow. He also brought out a pair of long-toed shoes, of which the one was blue and the other green.

'I got these,' he said, 'last Christmas for my coachman, who is a bit of a wag. You can wear them in the meantime.'

Mortimer gasped and trembled; he placed his hands on the toilet-table to steady himself and tried to speak, but passion choked him.

'Don't you like the dress?' asked Jamieson.

'No,' began Mortimer, but he could get no further.

'Give it a trial,' said Jamieson, turning to the wardrobe to select a dress for himself.

'Come,' he said, having made his choice and finding Mortimer's position unchanged, 'don't be sulky.'

With perfect good-humour he took a riding-whip from a peg, and switching the air looked at himself in one of the mirrors, and remarked to his reflection, "If I couldn't control my passions, I wouldn't like to

be your fool, my liege, since you claim the ancient
right of chastisement. No, my liege, I shouldn't like
to come under your whip, for I'll be bound you could
lay it on with any beadle or drum-major of them
all.'

Mortimer tried to swallow his passion at one
gulp, but it stuck in his throat for hours after.
Shuddering, he divested himself of his pepper-and-
salt and pulled on the red-and-yellow. As the
coachman for whom the dress had been made was
almost as tall as his master, Mortimer had considerable difficulty in disposing of the superfluous cloth.
The waist of the coat girded his thighs, the scalloped
skirt came below his knees, and half a foot of the
sleeve had to be rolled back, while the peak of it
depended from his wrist. As for the tights, they
had also to be rolled up, and they were so wide for
him that his legs looked as if some malicious malady
had destroyed the flesh, leaving the shrivelled skin
flapping about the bones. The cap and bells fitted
him well, his head being disproportionately big, but
the shoes stuck out behind as well as in front,
looking like a pair of rockers. He bore a strong
resemblance to a Brahmapootra cock. A careful
observation of the Brahmapootra cock might lead
one who knew no better to surmise that he is simply

a good-sized Spanish fowl, plucked alive by boys, coated with mud, and re-feathered in a hurry; his dress seems about to forsake him, and he shuffles along with his plumes coming down among his toes in evident dread of finding himself suddenly a two-legged animal without feathers. Some such idea as this crossed the Provost's mind as he contemplated Mortimer — a gigantic toy Brahmapootra cock mounted on rockers. Laughing, he pushed the little man among the mirrors, and Mortimer beheld himself from all points of view, and sank on the floor aghast and ashamed. His misery was complete when he turned his eyes on Jamieson, for he had apparelled himself magnificently in the fashion of the early part of Henry VIII's reign. He wore a plaited shirt embroidered with gold, and a small ruff; a coat of violet-coloured velvet, damasked with gold, the sleeves and breast slashed and puffed with cloth of gold and ornamented with rubies; his hose, which were of white knitted silk, extended, in accordance with the fashion he had adopted, from his waist to his feet; and he was shod with velvet buskins of the same colour as his coat, slashed and puffed with gold.

'No!' cried Mortimer, rising to his feet with tears in his eyes. 'What have I done, what have I said to merit this?'

His eloquence forsook him and the Provost marched him down to the hall, saying as the big shoes clattered on the steps, 'Good cousin Cosmo, you will come to like these garments in time. It is what every one wants, and is glad of ultimately,

however much he may rebel at first—to be shaken into a uniform; you are thrice lucky in getting the livery which is required to complete your character.'

Mortimer was unable to reply.

At dinner Jamieson was restless and silent; he

ate little and took no wine. He paid no attention
to Mortimer who, having recovered the use of his
tongue, kept up a constant muttering from the soup
to the salad, much to the amusement of the servants.
His smothered ejaculations were almost inaudible at
the start. Words and phrases, such as 'annuitant—
culture—literary ability—wretched provosts—incapable of greatness,' accompanied by fierce glances to
right and left, were distinguishable between the
spoonfuls of soup; but it was not until several
glasses of sherry and Jamieson's want of attention
had roused his courage that Mortimer's soliloquy got
fairly under weigh. Even then, although emphatic
enough, it was still suppressed: this added to its
intensity, but it did not become fluent till the end of
the dinner. A speech punctuated with potatoes and
pigeon-pie and roast meat, with dashes of sherry and
champagne, with periods of mastication and paren-
theses of silence, may be brilliant, but it cannot be
smooth.

'I'm not a hero—no!' he said, with a withering
glance at the cook. 'I don't think an annuitant
could be a hero.' Here he drank some champagne
and, taking a sight across the rim of his glass, plunged
his eyes into the coachman. 'But it doesn't follow
that a great man must be a hero. Hamlet,' he

specially informed the astonished boy in buttons,
' was a great man, but he wasn't a hero. The difference between great men and heroes is that great
men are wise and heroes are fools. Nelson was a
hero; Wellington was a great man. Heroes,' he
pointedly assured the maid who had served the
whisky at lunch, ' are eccentric ; heroism is eccentricity. That,' he explained to the gardener, ' is an
epigram.' He then devoted fully two minutes of
concentrated attention to a succulent slice of the
undercut. ' Greatness is humble, it is submissive ;
heroism is aggressive and arrogant.' Here he stole
a glance at Jamieson, and finding that he wasn't
observed turned on the full blaze of his eyes and
hissed out, ' Provosts have frequently been heroes ;
annuitants never ! '

Thus he continued, gathering momentum until,
with a stalk of celery in one hand and a knife with
a piece of cheese on the point of it in the other, he
stood up and burst into a storm of eloquence and
self-contradiction.

' To be kidnapped in this way,' he cried, extend-
ing the knife with the button of cheese like a minia-
ture foil, and rapping the table with the stalk of
celery, ' and that by a miserable Provost, whose sole
excuse is that he is affected with softening of the

F

brain, is unendurable, except by a great man. I
have endured it. I have suffered myself to be clad
in this antique misfit without a murmur. I have
sat here the object of the scorn and laughter of
menials. I have drunk the wine and eaten the meat
of my persecutor with patience—and even with considerable enjoyment. I have made some remarks to
which he has paid no attention ; but I trust he is
listening now.'

An animated gesture at this point sent the button
of cheese flying down the table. In the heat of the
moment the speaker made a lunge after it with his
knife, but, of course, failed to capture it. Then,
with that sort of reflex action which is the cause of
many ludicrous doings on the part of orators, he
stabbed his celery-stalk, and holding it out trans-
fixed on the point of his knife continued his
deliverance.

' I say,' he shouted, 'that a hero pure and simple
is never a great man, but a great man may be a hero.
Heroism is thoughtless, and it is allowable for a
great man sometimes to be thoughtless, but he
must take care that his thoughtlessness is not mere
thoughtless thoughtlessness, as, indeed, it cannot be,
for great men are never thoughtless. I have submitted to the indignities which I have specified ; I

have borne them with meekness—I have even turned
the other cheek ; but I now wish to enter a protest
against the inhumanity of the treatment which I
have received ; and the easiest and most heroic
method open to me in present circumstances is to
pluck off this cap of ignominy, which like a red-hot
crown has seared my temples and kept up a jingling
which has nearly driven me mad, and flinging it on
the ground, as you now see, to trample it under foot
like an accursed thing, crushing the miserable bells
of it flat on the floor, as you now hear.'

Having stamped on the cap and bells with both
feet, Mortimer folded his arms and sat down in a
great and heroic attitude.

The Provost smiled faintly and clapped his hands
gently. 'Bravo!' he cried ; but he was so pre-
occupied that he had not understood a word of what
Mortimer had said. He was about to resume his
meditation when it struck him that he had better
compliment his fool.

'Cosmo,' he said, 'if I only make as good a king
as you do a clown we shall be celebrated. It is
natural,' he added, after a moment's thought, 'that
the revival of the Stuart dynasty should be accompanied by the revival of the court-jester ; and if I
have the temerity to think that I am destined to

be the agent of one of these revivals, it is a small
matter to believe that in you I have become
acquainted with the reviver of the other.'

Mortimer gnashed his teeth.   'Will you not
understand ?' he cried.   'However grotesque and
absurd my words and ways may be in your eyes,
I am thoroughly earnest in all I do and say.   To
try to make a fool of me as you are doing is ignoble
and unworthy of a king.'

This appeal passed unheeded, for Jamieson's
thoughts were far away.   He rose, and the servants
left the hall ceremoniously.   Then he poured out
a glass of wine for himself—the first he had taken—
drank a little of it, pressed his forehead with both
hands, and leant towards Mortimer.

'Cosmo,' he said, 'we must act.   Some one has
said that if a man has done nothing remarkable
before he is thirty he will be a nonentity all his
life.   I am twenty-eight ; I have done nothing yet
but dream and devise deeds.   In two years—in
one—in a month—a man might forestall the fatal
thirty.   We have two years, Cosmo ; and to-night
we will join issue with time.   I have told you some
of my schemes ; I discard them all for the simplest
and best, and the most adventurous.   It occurred to
me at dinner, and it is this : to start to-night, on

foot, we two, and take our chance. We know the
object with which we go forth, but nothing more.
What do you think of it? But that doesn't matter;
my mind is made up. I have not felt so light-
hearted since I ceased reading novels.'

'Saul,' said Mortimer incisively, 'went out to
seek his father's asses and found a kingdom ; when
asses go out seeking a kingdom they may be thankful
if they find thistles.'

'The event is nothing to me now,' said Jamieson.
'My resolve to undertake the expedition and the
certainty that I shall go through with it to a final
result—a gallows or a crown—is the cause of my
happiness.'

Mortimer shed tears of helpless anger as he
followed Jamieson to the study.

It was after ten when, with cloaks over their
fancy dresses, they went forth through the fields by
an unfrequented way. Mortimer had been allowed
to put on his own cap and boots, but he had been
compelled to buckle round his waist a sword of
lath. Jamieson carried a rapier, and had a pistol
stuck in his belt ; he, also, wore a modern hat and
boots. When they had passed out of sight of
Mintern they left the fields, intending to take to
the highway ; but as there was still a possibility

of meeting known persons, they walked in a wood which skirted the road.

'Cosmo,' said Ninian, 'is this not better than fishing ?'

Mortimer's answer was not forthcoming at once. He had felt the soothing influence of the walk

through the fields, and was inclined temporarily to accept the position as the only means of getting out of it. It was with some hesitation, however, and a tremor in his voice, for it was difficult for the little man even to appear to yield, that he said, 'How means your majesty—as sport, pleasure, or duty ?'

Ninian stood still a second and blushed with delight : it was the first time he had been addressed as a king.

'But which is it, Cosmo?' he asked. 'I should say it partakes of the nature of all three.'

'Your majesty is partly right,' said Mortimer, who was astonished to find himself enjoying the situation, 'and partly wrong. It partakes of the nature of all three for you; it partakes of the nature of none of them for me.'

'How is that, good Cosmo? I thought all lawful occupations came under one of these three heads. I admit you are the first, so far as I know, to make a distinction between sport and pleasure; but I believe such exists.'

'Exists, my liege! It is the only distinction which does exist,' cried Mortimer, whose skill in the invention of theories submission had restored. 'In comparison with it all other distinctions are moonshine. Pleasure is used erroneously to denote all employments in which a man spends money without the hope of a monetary or concrete return of any kind : all basking and lounging and doing nothing from which a man derives satisfaction; every method of taking one's ease—all annihilation of time by any means which is not work. But this definition includes sport.   Then, why have we the word sport ?   You see, there are the two words—there must be two things.   At first I thought pleasure was generic, and sport a species, but I now know better.   Sport, my lord, is any serious undertaking from which a man derives neither pleasure nor profit, and which he does not intend or expect to be either pleasant or profitable.   One example will do.   I fish.   Well, why do I fish ?   And, by the way, I believe I'm the first angler who ever asked himself that question.   I fish because others fish.   I fish because I got the present of a rod when I was a boy.   I fish because I am an annuitant and, having nothing to do, must kill time in some orthodox fashion.   I hate angling ; it tires my arm ; I run the hooks into my fingers, and get wet, and frequently catch colds, and never catch fish.   But it is my sport ; I massacre my fingers, but I also massacre time, and I am respected because I am a sportsman.   Oh, my liege, it takes great men to be sportsmen !   Do you think the world would yield them such deference if self-denial and self-sacrifice were not at the bottom of all sport? I tell you the world cares for nothing but self-denial.'

'But I know fishers,' said Ninian, while Mortimer

paused for breath, 'who take great pleasure in their sport.'

'A contradiction in terms, my lord. There's the theory: sport is a serious undertaking, neither pleasant nor profitable. You can't get over that. Where pleasure enters there is no sport. Those fishers who take pleasure in fishing have ceased to be sportsmen, because they have ceased to exercise self-denial. You see? There's nothing like theory.

'Then, good cousin, what is your theory of your share in the present undertaking?'

'My lord, my share in the present undertaking is not pleasant, because I don't like it; it is not duty, because it is not work, and there is no inner voice compelling me; it is not sport, because, although neither pleasant nor profitable, it is not voluntary. There is one other category under which it may come, and that is slavery. I am the captive of your wiles and the captive of your sword; you force me to do a thing against my will and without a wage; I am therefore your slave. Let us finish it, my liege. Shall I bow down that you may put your foot on my neck?'

'No, Cosmo, no; you shall not be my slave, because, as long as you are my jester, I'll give you a salary; I'll double your income, Cosmo. As to

your not liking it, I can't help that. No man is fit
to be a king who is not a consummate judge of men.
I have given you the one rôle for which you are fitted,
and you will thank me in time. You see, Cosmo,
there's the theory : a king must be a consummate
judge of men. Now, I am a king, therefore I have
judged you rightly. There's nothing like theory,
Cosmo.'

Mortimer was quite prepared to prove that it
altogether depended on who enunciated the theory,
but Ninian's intimation that he was to be paid so
handsomely changed the aspect of affairs.

'Cousin,' he said, availing himself of the jester's
privilege, and with a blandness equal to Ninian's, ' I
shall accept your theory when you give me the same
satisfaction as a king which I seem to give you as a
fool.'

'A fair bargain,' said Ninian. ' I own my task
will be arduous. I have made a study of my
ancestors, and I think I know what to avoid, but
what models to follow is another matter.'

' But your majesty has already contradicted yourself, in my hearing, in this very matter of conduct.'

' Have I, Cosmo ? It can be only a seeming
contradiction.'

' As irreconcilable as yes and no.'

' Let us hear it.'

' Your majesty, with a condescension worthy of your ancient race, stated your determination to govern according to modern constitutional ideas. How can you reconcile that with your intention to revive feudalism ? '

' I admit, Cosmo, that my ideas on this whole subject of government are nebulous ; but whatever they may or shall be it is my intention to proceed constitutionally—that is, to educate the people to my way of thinking either by the pen or by the sword.'

With such talk they beguiled the way until the moon rose, and Ninian began to grow moody. They still kept in the wood, in which there was a beaten path parallel to the high road. The moon's light fell here and there like splashes of silver on the trunks of the trees and the dark glossy leaves of the blaeberries. Fitful gusts of wind travelled over the wood. They were to be heard whispering far off among the tree-tops ; and as they came nearer the sound seemed hardly louder, but more distinct and intense, until they passed with a prolonged ' hush ! ' over the heads of the travellers into the road ; and there they fell silent. These night winds at first soothed Ninian, but their rapid recurrence began to trouble him, and without consulting Mortimer he left

the wood. Mortimer followed him promptly, and
they continued their journey in silence for some
time.

At length Ninian, throwing off his cloak and
hanging it over his arm—an action in which his
companion imitated him — approached close to
Cosmo, as if glad to feel the neighbourhood of
another mortal, and addressed him less cavalierly
than he had yet done.

'Cousin,' he said, 'this road which we took because
it was the first we came to leads to Tullibolton.
Strange as it may seem to you, I have never visited
Tullibolton House, nor made the acquaintance of
the Mortons. I don't know what has prevented my
doing so—and, indeed, it seems strange to myself—
but we shall go there to-night. It is destiny which
has directed our steps.'

'How far are we from Tullibolton?' asked
Mortimer.

'Half a mile.'

'Well, my liege, it's about half-past twelve just
now. What kind of reception from the Mortons of
Tullibolton do you imagine awaits two utter strangers
at this time of night, and in our guise too?'

'Cosmo,' said Ninian, 'we are here upon an
adventure, and we must follow the indications that

are given us. Worldly wisdom, of which your
remark savours, is totally foreign to our undertaking, as to all great undertakings. Nothing valiant,
nothing noble, nothing great, was ever done by men
who counted the cost. In the small matter of our
visit to Tullibolton we have nothing to do with the
reception which awaits us. We feel constrained to
go there, and we go.'

'What sound is that?' cried Mortimer.

'I hear nothing,' said Ninian.

'I thought I heard riders in front, but I must
have been mistaken.'

'Mahomet's first converts were his relations,' said
Ninian, quickening his pace. 'I shall go to Tullibolton as a king; there must be no compromise
now.'

He strode along at such a rate that Mortimer,
having to trot in order to keep up with him, was
about to protest, when they were brought to a stand-
still by a cry of 'Halt.' At the same moment a
horse leapt from the shadow of some trees into the
road, and its rider, presenting a revolver, demanded
in a sweet voice their money or their lives.

Ninian instantly drew his pistol from his belt,
cocked it, and had almost fired when he observed
that the rider was a woman.

'Lady,' he said, still covering her with his pistol, 'if you need money I will give it you.'

He thought she might be in debt, as young ladies will sometimes be, and was now making a desperate attempt to get her account settled.

'Here's another!' gasped Mortimer, drawing his wooden sword and pressing close to Ninian, as a second amazon appeared from the shadow.

'You've lost, Marjory,' she said.

'Or won, aunt,' said the first, putting away her revolver and bending down to see Ninian, whose violet velvet and white silk made him a notable figure in the moonlight. She scanned him from top to toe, and her eyes rested long on his. Then she sat up in a hurry with a deep blush covering her face and neck. She had been surprised into her scrutiny of Ninian; it was his steady devouring gaze that recalled her to herself.

'I am the king,' said Ninian. 'Who are you?'

Marjory, amazed, made no answer; but her aunt, thinking that they dealt with masqueraders, replied for her.

'This is Miss Marjory Morton of Tullibolton.'

'Fair cousin,' said Ninian, more pleased than surprised, 'this is a happy meeting, for we are on our way to Tullibolton.'

'Aunt, come here,' said Marjory, turning her horse and riding forward a few yards.

'What shall I say?' she asked, when her aunt had joined her.

'Nothing,' was the answer. 'Ride straight home now. They are evidently bad men from Edinburgh or Glasgow on a holiday—and inferior too, I've no doubt.'

'I think I'll bid them welcome,' said Marjory, who had ridden off not so much to consult her aunt as to make up her mind; she was one of those to whom motion is necessary when a rapid decision is required. 'Yes, I'll invite them.'

'You will do a very wrong thing, then,' said her aunt.

'Not at all. He who calls himself the king is a gentleman every way; I saw it in his eyes.' She rode back, accompanied by her aunt, who vainly whispered dissuasive arguments.

'Gentlemen,' said Marjory, 'you will be welcome to Tullibolton. I think we shall have explanations to make to each other. You know the way?'

'Quite well, fair cousin,' said Ninian.

'We shall ride on, then, to prepare for your coming.'

'A thousand thanks,' said Ninian.

' Well ! ' exclaimed Mortimer, as the ladies rode away.

' Well ? ' queried Ninian.

' Nothing,' said Mortimer, shaking his head from side to side, and up and down, and looking unutterable theories.

CHAPTER IV

THOMSINA MERCER

WHEN Ninian and Cosmo entered the drawing-
room of Tullibolton House its sole occupant was the
elder of the two women. She sat where shaded
lamps half hid her face, and showed to best advantage the remains of her beauty. She had a fan,
which was excusable after her ride, and she played
it with some grace, varying the light and shade of
the lamps. She wore her riding-habit, and it became her well. Her face, even in the subdued light,
looked fully thirty-five, but her figure seemed much
younger. All this Cosmo took in at a glance, after
she had bowed them to a seat, and his inner voice
said, ' She's well preserved ; over forty ; face, a little
gone ; body, good—always the way with unmarried
women. Theory again. Faces of matrons last
longer than their figures ; figures of single women
last longer than their faces.'

'Gentlemen,' said the unconscious object of this criticism, 'I hardly know what to say, my niece is so wilful.'

'Madam,' began Mortimer.

'Peace, fool,' said Ninian.

Mortimer, always red-hot, turned to white heat, and ground his teeth. His post was to be no sinecure, that was evident.

It was well enough when they were alone, but he questioned if £400 a year was at all an equivalent for the indignity of being called 'fool' at Ninian's pleasure. He set himself to think the matter out.

'Madam,' continued Ninian, 'nothing in the whole course of my life has given me greater pleasure than this meeting.'

'I am sorry that it gives you so much pleasure, for my niece is acting very foolishly, I think. She will not be here for a minute or two yet, and if you are gentlemen you will leave the house before she comes.'

'How, madam! would you dictate to me?' said Ninian haughtily.

This rather disconcerted the lady, and she looked to Cosmo for help; but he was also unprepared for such rigorous absolutism.

'If Miss Morton,' said Ninian more graciously,
'requests our withdrawal, we shall comply.'

Nothing was said to this, so Ninian leant back
with his arms folded and stared at the ceiling. The
lady opened and shut her fan, and tapped the floor
with her foot, and Mortimer shifted about in his
chair until Marjory entered the room.

Her riding-habit had been changed for a costume
which she had worn a fortnight before at a ball in
Perth : a close-bodied gown of brocaded cream-
coloured silk with tight sleeves, and a gorget ruff
enclosing her head like an open casket, or the cup
of a flower ; her head-dress was a copy of that
commonly associated with Mary, Queen of Scots,
although the rest of her costume was more than half
a century later—after the style of Henrietta Maria.
She was under the average height for women, and
her figure was girlish ; she had just turned eighteen.
Her dark brown hair tinged with gold about the
temples hung in thick natural curls a little below
her shoulders. The lustre of health glowed in her
pale face. Her chin was broad, and her mouth large
and well shaped ; the lips of a dazzling red—the
effect of the pallor in which they shone ; her nose
was small, but straight ; her eyes dark blue, and
inclining to the almond-shape ; the eye-lashes long

and heavy ; the eye - brows straight and lightly marked ; the forehead broad and low.

' Balzac,' remarked Mortimer to himself, having rapidly appreciated all Marjory's points, ' Balzac says that there are a hundred ways of being a blonde, but only one of being a brunette. There is something in it, for I never saw a brunette like this before ; she proves the rule.'

Ninian rose as she walked up the room and gave her his hand, which she took with a blush and a sweeping curtsey. She sat on a couch, and he placed his chair beside her.

' Well, Marjory,' said her aunt, rising, ' you've done all you said you would do, and I hope you're satisfied. I think you'd better go to bed now.'

' No, aunt, I couldn't sleep. You know quite well I never do in these hot nights.'

' Then what are you going to do ? '

' I think we are going to talk,' said Marjory, turning towards Ninian.

' I have much to say,' said he.

' But this is folly and madness. I will not countenance it,' said her aunt, marching to the door.

' Cousin,' said Mortimer, ' you had better———'

' Go to the kitchen, fool,' said Ninian. ' To the kitchen with you ! '

' Revenge!' cried Mortimer.

'You are to leave the room,' said Ninian, going towards Mortimer, who retreated to the door. Marjory's aunt went out quickly, anticipating violence, and Ninian pushed Mortimer after her, saying as he closed the door, ' Let no one come here till I ring the bell.'

' This is the last straw!' cried Mortimer; 'the last straw!'

Marjory had risen also, and faced Ninian as he turned from the door. She had intended to remonstrate, but the blaze of his eyes and the power in his expression and gesture stopped her. All she said was, ' You see, I have put on a fancy dress too.'

But we require to follow Mortimer in the meantime.

'Don't,' he said, withholding Marjory's aunt, who
was about to reopen the drawing-room door. 'The
man's mad.'

'But my niece!' exclaimed the lady.

'Must take care of herself.'

'It is her fault, certainly.'

'Will you allow me to explain how I became
entangled with this insane fool?'

'Yes; come in here.'

She led the way into a little sitting-room and
lit the gas, and Mortimer and she sat down
together.

'Whom have I the pleasure of addressing?'
asked the lady.

After Ninian's free and easy style Mortimer was
delighted with this formality. 'Mr. Cosmo Mortimer,'
he replied. 'To whom have I the honour of making
myself known?'

'Miss Thomsina Mercer,' said the lady.

'Shocking!' cried Mortimer, surprised at once out
of his ceremony. 'My dear lady, I suppose you
know that Mercer is a provostal name; half the old
provosts of Perth were Mercers.'

'They were my ancestors,' said Miss Mercer.

'And Thomsina!' said Mortimer, with horror in
his voice ; 'have you not found the name a terrible
infliction ? '

'What do you mean, sir?' said Thomsina, slapping
her fan together angrily.

'Pardon, pardon!' cried Mortimer. 'You must
understand I have a theory of names, which
tells me that you would fain be eccentric, but
you are tied by a middle-class mode of thinking.
You——'

'Mr. Mortimer, is it you or your master who is
mad ? My name is no concern of yours. Tell me
what is the meaning of this night-wandering and
masquerading.'

Mortimer plunged into a narrative of his adventures since his arrival in Mintern ; and Miss Mercer,
much impressed with the story, and in Mr. Mortimer's
favour, listened to the end without interrupting him.

'How much truth,' asked Mortimer, when he had
done, 'or is there any, in this story of the Chevalier
de St. George ? '

'I never heard it before,' said Miss Mercer ; 'but
I believe I know the source of it, and I shall tell you.
But is it not terrible, when you think of it, Mr.
Mortimer ? Here are we talking at half-past one
o'clock in the morning as unconcernedly and as

intimately as if it were broad daylight and we had known each other for twenty years ! But I am done with my niece henceforth, her and her whims. She is a most dreadful girl, Mr. Mortimer, and is the cause of the gravest anxiety to her relations. We don't know how or when it got there, but there is bad blood in the family, Mr. Mortimer. It appears at irregular intervals, and the first known appearance of it must, I think, have given rise to this theory of Mr. Jamieson's about the Chevalier de St. George. The Marjory Morton of that time certainly had a son who was called James Jamieson, but, Mr. Mortimer, so was his father before him. He was the coachman, and Marjory ran off with him to Gretna Green. He was killed at Sheriffmuir, and she returned to her father. Her son is the ancestor of the Provost of Mintern. The Mortons have always ignored the Jamiesons, though quite aware of their existence. I don't suppose that a single Morton has been in Mintern for several generations. It was not to be thought of while the shop filled one side of the principal square, and the "Dunmyatt Whisky" in tartan letters appeared wherever a bill could be stuck ; and still less now that a Jamieson is Provost. What would my brother-in-law say if he knew who was in the house at this moment ? '

'He is a thorough-going impostor, then, this diamond-making Provost?'

'Undoubtedly.'

'I shall expose him in the newspapers.'

'Will you? In what paper?'

'I don't know; but I shall do it. Justice as well as vengeance requires it.'

'The *Mintern Gazette* would be glad of any attack on the Provost; and I think you would be perfectly justified, Mr. Mortimer, you, a man of position, of means, and of culture, forced to submit to the indignities you have mentioned, in giving him a thorough scarifying.'

'I'll scarify him—I'll skin him alive!' said Mortimer. 'I'll do it at once. When is the paper published?'

'On Saturday, so there is no hurry.'

'This is Thursday—no, Friday morning. There's not much time to lose.'

'You must get a sleep first, Mr. Mortimer. I am certain my brother-in-law would esteem it an honour to have you in Tullibolton House.'

Mortimer bowed profoundly.

'I was accounting to you as far as possible,' continued Miss Mercer, 'for Marjory's absurdities, to call them by a gentle name. There have been two

Marjories between the one that married the coachman and the present one. The Maggies, the Janets,
the Lizzies of the family have all been jewels of
women, but in the Marjories the bad blood appears.
One of them married her father's under-gardener, and
the other eloped with a commercial traveller. What
this one will do heaven only knows! You see how
she behaves. Imagine, Mr. Mortimer! We had a
long discussion about the men of the present genera-
tion—my niece and I. It lasted till eleven o'clock.
She declared that there wasn't a spark of chivalry
left among them ; that the getting hold of money
and the spending it on themselves was all they lived
for ; that they were all cowards—and I'm sure I
don't remember all she said. I reminded her of
Gordon, but she burst out, "Why isn't every man a
Gordon ?" and she wouldn't listen to me. She said
the women were fools and cowards too, and instanced
me, Mr. Mortimer, if you please, because with my
£200 a year I didn't " do something." . She challenged
me to ride with her a mile along the road at midnight. I was angry and accepted the challenge, not
foreseeing the disastrous results—I mean, for her.
For myself I have to thank this mad-brained expedition, because it has gained me your acquaintance,
Mr. Mortimer.'

'I could almost forgive Jamieson's insults on the same account, madam,' said Mortimer.

The pair becked and bowed, and Thomsina blushed, and Mortimer's vanity was gratified after the rough usage it had received at the hands of the Provost.

'I wasn't to be outdone,' continued Thomsina, 'so I said to Marjory, "You have bragged a deal. Will you take a pistol with you, and if we meet one of these cowardly men demand his money or his life?" "I will," she said, "and he'll give me his money or run away." "He won't," I said. "If he doesn't," says she, firing up, "I'll marry him, or give you my diamond brooch."'

'Oho!' cried Mortimer. 'I understand what you two said to each other now. Didn't you say, "You've lost, Marjory," and she answered, "Or won, aunt"?'

'Exactly.'

'And would she marry the Provost, do you think.'

'A very likely thing, if for no other reason than to spite her family.'

'She must be a terrible creature.'

'She is, indeed, Mr. Mortimer. The rest of the family, except her father, are in Switzerland; but she wouldn't go. She said she had made a vow never to leave Scotland again, and nothing would move her. She couldn't be left here alone, so I was told off to watch her, in the hope, as she hates me, that she would break her absurd vow. But no ; so here we are.'

'A very remarkable girl; very. Marjory Morton —a difficult name to deal with.'

'And a difficult woman, Mr. Mortimer.'

'Evidently.'

'Now, what is to be done ? '

'Where's her father ? '

'In London. He wishes to enter Parliament at next election, and he is endeavouring to secure the support of the leaders.'

'Then he must be telegraphed for at once.'

'That's my idea too.'

'Miss Mercer, you are a woman of intellect and of daring. How to reconcile these qualities with your name, if you will allow me the remark, is more than I can say in the meantime ; but I shall work out the problem.'

'Thank you,' said Thomsina drily.

'I see,' said Mortimer, 'that it is a delicate subject with you, and I do not wonder at it. Thomsina Mercer is, to all appearance, a name incapable of greatness. Now, there are elements of greatness in

your character.   Why not do as other women with
unfortunate names have done?   Look at Marian
Evans.   Do you think these paltry syllables would
have developed the genius of George Eliot?   But
I'll go thoroughly into the matter at leisure.   Now,
if you give me writing materials I'll pen an exposure
of this wretched impostor and take it to Mintern at
once.'

'And the telegram?'

'I'll look after that too.'

'But we always send our telegrams from Perth.
It's quite as near as Mintern.   My brother-in-law
will be scandalised at receiving a telegram from
Mintern.'

'Does he carry his resentment so far as that?'

'He is terribly touchy on the point.   His health
has never been what it was since the "Dunmyatt
Whisky" came out.'

'I like him—I like a man who can be extreme.
Depend upon it, Miss Mercer—but what is his first
name?'

'Andrew.'

'A good name, though common.   There is the
possibility of a sound reputation in Andrew Morton,
especially if he narrows himself down to a point, as
I've no doubt he will.   He will never be a great

statesman, but he would make a very good chairman of committees.'

Miss Mercer again invited Mortimer to take some rest, but he declared he couldn't. Half bewildered and half offended she took him to the library, where he soon wrought himself to a white heat over his paper for the *Mintern Gazette*.

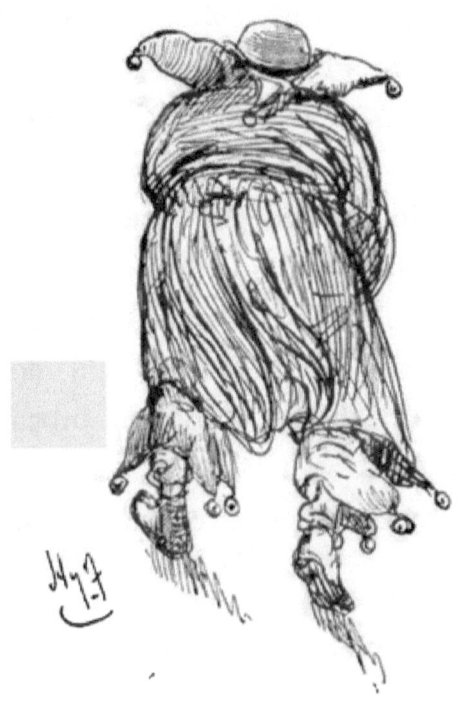

CHAPTER V

MARJORY MORTON

MARJORY MORTON was capable of making a good remark in trying circumstances, and in a shipwreck or a fire would have been cool among the coolest. The novelty of her midnight adventure excited her, but the press of ideas made her feel as if she were in a blind alley ; hence the inferiority of her remark when she was alone with Ninian, 'You see I have put on a fancy dress too.'

'Miss Morton,' he began, and stopped. He was affected in the same way as Marjory, though in a less degree. He pressed his head with both hands and shook back his hair. In the action he caught a glimpse of himself in the mirror and felt at once what was wrong. *Miss* Morton did not suit his violet velvet and white silk, or her brocaded gown and pearled head-dress.

'Lady,' he said, lingering on the word, ' my time

is brief, but I must have you on my side, though I spend the night in persuading you.'

He led her to the couch, and took the chair he had placed beside it. He then stated his claim to the crown of Britain, and told her more powerfully than he had told Mortimer of his struggles with himself. When he had finished he rose and said, ' Do you acknowledge me ? '

' I do not know,' said Marjory, looking at the floor with knitted brows.

' I am sorry,' said Ninian ; ' I feel that my fate depends on you. If you acknowledge me I shall go on hopefully ; if not, in despair.'

' Why ? '

' If you do not acknowledge me, who will ? Because you have faith in romance, and are in sympathy with all noble aspiration, I think you have sympathy with me.'

' I have,' she said musingly. ' I am sick of the life I have led, and mean to lead it no more ; and I love Scotland as I think nobody else loves it now—as Burns loved it, and Scott loved it.'

She was anxious to speak if this strange handsome man with his dark eyes and deep tender voice would only help her. She had never before talked

H

with any one to whom she felt she could explain herself.   He did help her.

'So do I,' he said.   'I would be content to be king of Scotland and leave the rest of the Empire to the House, of Brunswick.   But it would require to be repeopled.   They say there are more Scotchmen in London than there are in Edinburgh.   I would bring all these prodigals back, and from the colonies, and America.'

'It is shameful,' she burst out, 'how Scotchmen forsake their country!   I am almost a socialist in some things, but I would preserve nationalities. My ambition comes far short of yours, still it is high-flown enough.   I would like to see Edinburgh once more the home of the Scotch nobility; to see it a literary centre rivalling London and Paris.   And it could be done so easily.   If the Duke of Weimar with his small income could gather together Goethe, Schiller, and the wit and wisdom of Germany, surely a Scotch nobleman could gather about him in Edinburgh all the eminent Scotchmen.   That would make us a nation once more.'

'But a king would be infinitely better,' said Ninian.

'Perhaps.'

'It is certain.   When they cut off my great

ancestor's head they did not know that they struck
a blow at England and Scotland, at every nation on
the face of the earth.   Monarchy and nationality are
the head and the body.   There are Frenchmen, but
no French nation ; Americans, but no American
nation.   Wherever there is a monarch there is a
nation ; and the more absolute the monarchy the
more marked the nationality.   I will be king of
Scotland—I will be king of Scotland.'

He advanced to within a foot of her and stood,
his hands before him, one holding the other by the
wrist.   She looked up, and seemed unable to meet
his glance.

'Am I the king ? ' he asked under his breath.

'I do not know.'

He turned from her and paced the room.   She
looked at his feet, then her eyes gradually crept up
to his face.   She was still watching the rapid change
of expression that crossed it when he came towards
her again and caught her glance.   This time she
returned his gaze.

'I *am* the king,' he said.

'But '— she hesitated —' the proof ? '

'Do you think that I could be king ? '

'Yes.'

'Then you must not doubt my word.'

'But there may be a mistake.'

'Impossible; I have the documents; you shall see them.'

She bowed and said nothing, and he stood looking at her.   Her eyes fell, and were again raised with an inquiring glance which Ninian understood.

'I haven't brought them with me,' he said; 'but I can get them.   To-night!—I will get them to-night. I ought to have them with me.   Where is my fool?'

'Oh, not to-night!' she said.

'He can ride.   You will lend him a horse.'

He was about to ring when Marjory said, 'Do not; there is no one to answer.   I will go for him.'

It is well to note that the interview between Marjory and Ninian had been of some duration.   Long pauses had occurred; and Ninian's account of himself, omitted in our narrative, took up a considerable time.

Marjory returned in a few minutes with Miss Mercer, whom she had found dozing in an armchair in the library.

'Where is my fool?' said Ninian.

'Mr. Mortimer,' said Thomsina with dignity, 'has left Tullibolton.'

'Without my permission!   The knave!   Where has he gone?'

'To Mintern.'

' When did the rascal go ? '

Thomsina gave no answer.

' Do you hear ?   When did he go ? '

' Sir,' said Thomsina, with an oblique motion of the head and a prolonged droop and gradual up-heaval of the eyelids, ' I am not in the habit of being talked to in this way, nor of hearing my personal friends denominated rascals.'

' I was not aware that you knew Cosmo.'

' I do know him now,' she said.   ' He is a gentleman of birth and breeding, for whom I have a great respect.'

' Why, you've only known him an hour,' said Marjory.

' How long have you, mademoiselle, known this person ? '

Thomsina indicated Ninian with another oblique gesture of disdain.   To her delight she found she had delivered a home-thrust, for her niece blushed and said nothing.

' My good woman,' said Ninian, ' when did Cosmo go ? '

' Mademoiselle ' is a term of reproach in Scotland, more stinging even than ' person ' ; but it is safer to call a French general a liar than to address any female as ' My good woman.'

'You are a crack-brained, low-born fellow,' said
Thomsina, passing to the door with extreme obliquity.
'I laugh at you and scorn you, and you will be the
laughing-stock and scorn of the world before the
week's out. And you, Marjory!—you dupe, you
fool, you can only save your character by bidding
him go. I wash my hands of you.' She left the
room with a slow step, closing the door softly behind
her—an affectation of coolness which failed to ex-
asperate either Ninian or Marjory.

'The flight of Cosmo,' said Ninian, 'is rather
annoying. But why should it trouble me? If he
does as he threatened it will give me publicity, and
once in the newspapers there is no halting, no
turning back. I should like to go to bed now, if
you please. To-morrow I will get the documents.'

Marjory in silence showed him to a bedroom, and
in a few minutes he was sound asleep; but she
walked her room till the cocks were crowing and
the sun was above the hills, then she burst into tears
and threw herself upon her bed. She had hardly
done so when some one passed her room stealthily
and went downstairs. Without any hesitation she
followed and found Ninian opening the front door.

'Why do you steal away like this?' she asked.

He blushed and hung his head.

'I trusted you,' she said, without any clear meaning in her mind.

'Lady, I am a coward,' said Ninian. 'Let me
go.'

'Go!'

'But that is neither the word nor the tone which
a man obeys.'

'I thought you were a coward.'

'I am,' he said, with humility. 'I am flying
from temptation instead of facing it.'

'Temptation!'

'Yes. What was the besetting sin of the Stuarts?'

Marjory considered her answer: she was not
going to be silenced by plain speaking.

'Random love,' she said.

'No,' said Ninian, talking rapidly, 'it was not
that, but an unmanly yielding to the influence of
women. Henrietta Maria was much more fatal to
Charles I. than all his Nell Gwyns to the Merry
Monarch. Think of Flora Macdonald. Prince
Charles should have died at Culloden; failing that
he should have given himself up. His death on the
scaffold would have been the salvation of his house;
and he would have been beheaded in spite of his
cowardice had not that woman protected him. I
have all the Stuarts' passionate adoration of woman

unsullied, and were I not a king I would make some woman happy ; but a king, least of all a Stuart king, should never love.'

'But why should you leave the house without bidding me good-bye ? '

'Lady, you torture me. I dreamt of you. You were my wife. We lived in Holyrood ; and our

rooms were filled nightly by poets and painters, philosophers and men of science. Edinburgh was the intellectual capital of the world ; and though I was not the king you were queen. I am tempted to turn aside from my path ; but I am not fit to be king if I cannot at least fly from temptation. I take it that destiny brought us together to try me.'

'And me ? ' said Marjory.

'You!' exclaimed Ninian, stunned.   'I never thought of you.'

'Your egotism is sublime,' said Marjory.

'Farewell,' said Ninian, turning from her suddenly.   He ran away at the top of his speed, and did not slacken it until he was out of Marjory's sight. She watched him vanishing and stretched out her hands after him.

CHAPTER VI

COSMO AND THOMSINA

THE first visitor on Friday morning at the office of the *Mintern Gazette* was Cosmo Mortimer, dressed in his own serviceable pepper-and-salt, sleepy looking and rather pale for him, but ready as ever at a moment's notice to theorise on anything. On arriving at the Provost's house he had persuaded the servants that he was on their master's business. He had slept for an hour or two; at eight he had breakfasted; at half-past eight he had removed his traps to the Mintern Arms; and at nine he was astonishing Mr. Adie, the editor of the *Mintern Gazette,* with the history and theory of Ninian Jamieson.

'And now, sir,' he said, 'having made an end of my introductory remarks, I come to the object of my visit. I have here in the shape of a letter to you an exposure of this madman couched in the

most sarcastic terms.   It will rejoice the heart of all
his enemies, and be gall and wormwood to his
friends.   Every word of it stings, and I have signed
it "Castigator."   I believe in anonymity.   The
ministers of Nature's justice are anonymous—flood,
fire, famine, and fever—and so am I, in a double sense.'
Cosmo was thinking of a certain Hugh Smith.

'Let me see it,' said the editor drily.

Cosmo handed over the letter.

'On second thoughts, it's no use,' said the editor,
returning the manuscript without looking at it.   'I
have persistently attacked the Provost because I
think him a most unsuitable man——'

'Error, error!' burst in Cosmo.   'Magistracy is
what nature intended him for.   Names, my dear
sir——'

'I was saying,' resumed the editor, regardless of
the interruption, 'that Jamieson is totally unfitted for
the provostship, but I'm going to leave him alone in
the meantime, as I never hit a man when he's down.'

'Down!' exclaimed Mortimer.

'Yes,' said the editor, picking up a proof which
he had been correcting when Mortimer entered the
shop,—'down.   See.'

Mortimer read the paragraph which the editor
indicated.

'That's the full meaning of the name, is it?' he cried in great excitement. 'This is a new light. Good-morning, sir, and thank you.'

'A new light!' he repeated as he hurried out of the shop. 'Tullibolton House,' he said to the driver, as he got into a cab. 'A new light!' he repeated to himself.

Miss Mercer was at breakfast when he arrived.

'Mr. Mortimer!' she exclaimed. 'I am so glad to see you again, and in your own clothes.'

'Madam,' said Mortimer, 'give me a cup of tea.'

'Certainly, Mr. Mortimer. And how did you get on with the editor?'

'Madam, let me drink the tea.'

'Surely, Mr. Mortimer, surely. You must be tired. How thoughtless of me!'

'Madam,' said Mortimer, having taken the tea at a draught, 'I have news. There is something besides eccentricity in the name Ninian. Jamieson I analysed correctly—commercial prosperity and civic honour; but I failed with Ninian, because I have hitherto omitted in my theory an element which must enter into the composition of many names. Besides eccentricity Ninian spells—what do you think?—bankruptcy.'

'You startle me, Mr. Mortimer.'

' The Provost is to-day a pauper.'

' How shocking ! I understood he was very rich.'

' He was, madam, in affluent circumstances. To-day he hasn't a penny.'

' Dear me ! What has brought about this change ? '

' He has been speculating. I know no details, but it is certain he is bankrupt. I should like to see him now. I shall exult in his fall ; I shall crow over him to his face. Lead me to him, madam, if you please.'

' He is not here.'

' Not here ! '

' No, he went away early in the morning.'

' Where has he gone ? '

' I don't know.'

' Does Miss Morton know ? '

' I don't think so.'

' But he has certainly left Tullibolton ? '

' There's no doubt of it.'

' So much the better—so much the better ! He will go about making a fool of himself all the longer, for I would have told him of his bankruptcy had I seen him—I couldn't have helped it ; and that would have put an end to his campaign at once.'

' Did you telegraph for Mr. Morton ? '

'I forgot all about it, madam.'

'I'm just as glad since Jamieson has gone away of his own accord. However, I shall write Mr. Morton myself now, giving up all charge of Marjory. After last night what she needs is a strait-jacket and douche-baths ; an aunt is no check on her, Mr. Mortimer.'

'And what will *you* do then, madam ? '

'I'm sure I don't know, Mr. Mortimer. My relations are tired of me long ago, and as soon as I cease to be useful to them they will cast me on the world without a home or a friend—with nothing but my £200 a year.'

'Do not despond, Miss Mercer. In my opinion it is desirable that you should be severed from your friends and relations, because you can change your name.'

'Oh, Mr. Mortimer ! '

'But you can. It doesn't cost a very great deal, and you can go at once among strangers who will never know. To attempt a change of name among one's intimates is simply to stick in your hat, as it were, " Jokes shot here." '

'Then,' said Thomsina falteringly, 'you mean that I should change my name myself.'

'Certainly, madam. I changed mine. My

patronymic was simply fatal to greatness, and my Christian name a libel ; I was called Hugh Smith ; but I refused to be the victim of such a dastardly conspiracy, and took my present name. You, madam, can do the same.'

'Oh, Mr. Mortimer!'

'You can. Have you any idea what you would like to be called?'

'Then,' said Thomsina, more falteringly, 'you do not mean that I should take your name. I thought you said I could "do the same."'

'If you like. The effect upon myself, madam, since I became Cosmo Mortimer more than surprises me. I am healthier, I am wiser, I am more courageous, I am better looking, and I believe, madam, that I have actually grown in stature half an inch, and I didn't change my name till I was thirty. But it doesn't follow that Mortimer would have the same effect on you as on me. Indeed, I think you'd better take something else.'

'You will excuse my question,' said Thomsina in a low voice, 'but the great interest you take in names and in me prompts it. What do you think of the ordinary method of changing women's names?'

'What is that?' asked Mortimer briskly.

'By marriage.'

'Ha!' said Mortimer, ' I am totally unable to say. Mrs. Shakespeare wasn't a great woman, but Lady William Russell was. There were three noteless Mrs. Miltons, but one Madame Roland, one Mrs. Carlyle. This is an exceedingly difficult aspect of the subject, and I should say it would be impossible

to arrive at a theory without personal experience. Not until I had changed my own name did I begin clearly to appreciate the immense importance of nomenclature. So, I should suppose, were I to take a wife I would, in time, understand the effect of a change of name by marriage in the characters of women.'

'It would be a very interesting study,' said Thomsina.

'It would indeed,' said Cosmo.

He pondered, while she cut a small finger of toast into a dozen pieces.

'Why did you never marry, Miss Mercer?' said Cosmo.

'Well,' she said, 'I think it was because of my name. Whoever would marry a woman called Thomsina! Besides I never cared for the men who wanted me, and the men didn't care for me whom I wanted.'

There was some calculation in this answer: the concession to Cosmo's theory in the first part of it, and the common sense of the second, were not without their result. Cosmo looked at her steadily and then said, 'You would like to be capable of greatness, Miss Mercer?'

'I would indeed, Mr. Mortimer.'

'And I should like to try it.'

'To try what, Mr. Mortimer?'

'Marriage.'

'Oh, Mr. Mortimer.'

'I should like to make a scientific study of the change in character produced in a woman by taking her husband's name. Mrs. Cosmo Mortimer,' he

murmured. 'Mrs. Cosmo Mortimer. Why, it
might develop genius in a rag-picker!—Madam,
will you be Mrs. Cosmo Mortimer?'

'Yes,' said Thomsina softly, but with a certain
fulness of affirmation. Cosmo stepped up promptly
and kissed her on the cheek, then he looked earnestly
into her eyes as if expecting to see signs of a change
in her character already. She dropped her eyelids
and laid her hand on his; he kissed her hand, and
resumed his seat; she mechanically finished her
toast, and he watched her in silence. Thomsina
grew very uncomfortable, and Cosmo was beginning
to think of something to say—usually a needless
preliminary with him—when Marjory entered the
room. She bowed to Cosmo and wished her aunt
good-morning.

'Good-morning, Marjory,' said Thomsina. 'The
diamond brooch is mine.'

'How so?'

'The Provost is bankrupt.'

'Bankrupt!'

'Yes,' said Thomsina. 'Wild as you are, you
will hardly wed a pauper.'

'Bankrupt!' repeated Marjory, sighing like one
before whom a beautiful vision fades away.

'I will wear the brooch at my marriage.'

'At your marriage!' said Marjory with wide eyes.

'Miss Morton,' said Cosmo, 'your aunt is to be Mrs. Cosmo Mortimer.'

'I wish you joy,' said Marjory, looking from one to the other, amazed and amused. Then she left the room, suppressing a laugh.

'Cosmo,' said Thomsina after she had gone, 'do you love me very much?'

'What!' cried Cosmo, starting from his seat. 'Do I love you? Love!—Madam, madam, do you know what love is?'

'Yes,' said Thomsina, 'I will love my husband.'

'Love your husband! Madam, such talk is intolerable between persons of our age.'

'Then, why do you wish to marry me?'

'I have told you, madam: to study the effect of my name upon you. I thought you understood that clearly. You see, you are a most suitable subject. You have lived for many years under an abominable name, by which your character has been reduced to zero, so that the slightest upward tendency will be visible at once. You are old enough—at least, I thought you were—to perceive the nonsense of love and all that sort of thing. I wish to marry you as an experiment in a science of which I am the discoverer—a science calculated to revolutionise the

world.   The name equates the character : raise the
power of the name and you raise that of the character.   Don't you see, man ?' cried Cosmo enthus-
iastically, forgetting the sex of his hearer.   'All the
sin and misery, the folly and madness of the world,
is the result of nomenclature.   Look here.   Take a
dozen burglars ; give them five years each, and let
them out again under their own names : ten of them
will be sentenced to ten years within as many months.
Take another dozen burglars, and let the Home
Secretary change their names ; he might call Sikes,
Wilberforce—Fagin, Howard—and so on ; give
them no punishment, no police supervision : I tell
you within six months every one of the twelve will
have honest money in the savings-bank—I know
it.   And the world in its heart knows it.   How
could it have produced the proverb " Call a man a
thief and he'll steal " if it didn't ?   And the Popes
know it.   Why else do they change their names on
their elevation ?   And titles !   Think of titles.
When you make a man a duke, do you think it
doesn't change his character ?   I tell you if you
were to take a small village in France and change
the names of all the inhabitants to Smith, Brown,
Jones, Robinson, and so on, within six months that
village would be dining on beef-steak and Bass's

beer and taking in the *Times*. The world's all
wrong from the Czar of Russia to the anarchist who
flings a bomb into a children's hospital. Look here,
man : call earth heaven, and raise the power of every
other name in proportion, and you would *have* heaven.'

'Then, Mr. Mortimer, you don't love me?'

'I should think not! I have no objection to the
word "love," either as a noun or as a verb, but I
have insuperable objections to what is understood by
love, and more especially to what women understand
by love. You see——'

'Mr. Mortimer,' said Miss Mercer, rising—and
anger made her beautiful,—'I am not a young
woman, and I am vain and foolish, but I will never
marry a man who thinks of love as you do. I long
to be a bride, and I long to be a wife, and to be a
mother, but I feel that all that is nothing to the love
of a man. I thank you, Mr. Mortimer, for the offer
of your *name*. Good-bye.'

She swept out of the room, as red as a rose and
as lovely as her niece. She sobbed for half an hour,
and then sought Marjory.

'You have been crying, aunt,' said Marjory.

'And so have you,' said Thomsina.

Quickly these two women, more than indifferent
before, found a way into each other's hearts.

CHAPTER VII

NINIAN AND MARJORY

Cosmo, disgusted with Thomsina's unscientific spirit, drove back to Mintern, soliloquising all the way.

'Women,' he said, 'are fools. The only hope for them is to change their appellation. Look at George Sand, George Eliot, Currer Bell! It was only by imagining themselves men that those women wrote their great novels ; and the softer sex cannot be hardened until the word "woman" is abolished, and the word "man" substituted for it. All children must be called boys, and all adults men. It's infallible. Change the name and you change the thing. There's no getting over that. I am astonished that the importance of theory has never been recognised. Make a generalisation, believe it, act upon it, and there you are!'

In this strain he continued until he arrived at the Mintern Arms. After lunch he went to fish, and lashed the water till five o'clock, catching nothing with much theoretical satisfaction. On his way home a voice hailed him. He looked behind, and saw a tall figure in a long waterproof running towards him. It was the Provost.

'Well, Cosmo,' said Ninian, when he came up to him, 'I hope you've had good sport.'

'I have,' said Cosmo. 'I hadn't a single rise, and I've caught a cold.'

'I'm very glad,' said Ninian, laughing. 'By the bye, have you any theory about putting your hand to the plough and turning back?'

'I have,' said Cosmo. 'I could expound it better, however, if you would give me the example that occurs to you.'

'It is myself. I am, as you see, returning, and you know how little is accomplished.'

'I must know why you are returning.'

'Certainly. I left Tullibolton House very early this morning and walked rapidly for two hours. Then I began to be hungry, so I went into a little cottage by the wayside and supped two plates of porridge which I found sitting on the kitchen table. I had just finished when a young couple came in together. The wife had made the porridge and then gone out for her husband, who was working in

a field at hand. They were too much surprised, and
even awed, to say anything. I apologised for the
liberty I had taken ; said they would be no losers
by me, and remembered that I hadn't a farthing.
This confused me a little, which the ploughman
observed. He said, " You'll be one o' these circus
billies, I'm thinkin' ; but there's naebody here gaun
tae laugh at your tricks. Pay doon a saxpence, or
come oot and fecht." Now, though I never went
twice a week to the Bois de Boulogne, I can box a
bit, Cosmo, so I accepted his challenge. One round
was sufficient, as the good fellow had no science ;
and I rather astonished him by holding his wife with
my left hand—for she attacked me tooth and nail—
while I settled him with my right. I cut off one of
my buttons and gave it to the woman, telling her it
was worth many sixpences, shook hands with her
husband, and went on my way. Something led me
to Dunmyatt, and I spent the forenoon on the top
of it. On the way down a new idea occurred to me.
Stirling Castle, which is the noblest feature in the
view from Dunmyatt, suggested it. " What a magnificent residence for a king !" I thought. You
know I am now going to confine my ambition to
Scotland. " From the windows of that palace a
Scottish king can look on half his realm, with the

broad Forth winding slowly to the Scottish sea.
Stirling Bridge and Bannockburn are at his feet. In
all the world there is no such home for a patriot
king.   Could I not take up my abode in the town,
form a party in the garrison, and seize the castle?
To be King of Scotland for one week, for one day
in Stirling Castle, with the block for a pillow at
night, would be worth more to me than any life
lived in this century."   I resolved to make the
attempt, and then came in the question of money
and of the proofs of my descent.   Could I go on as
I had started, and without my documents?   I could
write for some money, but in the meantime what
was I to do?   It was neither documents, however,
nor the money so much as a ring I had forgotten
that decided me.   As I could not bear to fail
ignominiously, or to perish meanly, I have provided
myself with poison in a ring.   I forgot it in the
hurry last night, and for that I have returned.   I
went down to Blairlogie, bought this old waterproof
with another button—it was necessary to hide my
dress as I had changed my plan—and here I am.
Now what do you think of my turning back?'

'I haven't got all the data,' said Cosmo.   'What
were you thinking of all the forenoon on the top of
Dunmyatt?'

'Ha! I was dreaming, dreaming.'

'Of what?'

'Of being king in Holyrood.'

'And as you came down the hill your dream changed to Stirling.'

'It did.'

'And who was your queen in this dream of yours?'

'My queen!' exclaimed Ninian, blushing.

'Of course. "Find the woman" is an ancient saying.'

'It's of no consequence. I've dreamt of hundreds of women in my life, and thought I loved some, but I'm a bachelor still.'

'I can tell who was your queen. It was Marjory Morton, and she is the cause of your turning back, and not your ring, or your documents, or the want of money. I will wager half my salary that you purpose setting out for Stirling to-night by way of Tullibolton House.'

'Cosmo, you are a wise fool. That is my intention. What do you think now?'

'That your turning back is fatal to your plan.'

'Why? Because of Marjory?'

'No; because of money. Had the desire to find a means of seeing Marjory again not suggested an errand back to Mintern you would have gone on, trusting to your pistol for an emergency such as you fear, without money and without documents, to *some* end. Now you have made money the basis of your plan, and you will fail—fail immediately.'

'Why do you think so?—But here we are at my house. You can explain yourself further when we go in.'

'I'm not going in.'

'Oh yes, you are!'

'But I have ordered dinner at the Mintern Arms.'

'Never mind. Come away. You must come.'

'Well,' thought Cosmo, 'I want to see how he takes his bankruptcy; but I'll submit to no more hectoring.'

Having satisfied his vanity with this resolution he accompanied Ninian. They entered at the back and passed through the kitchen.

'Is dinner ready?' Ninian asked.

'Yes, sir,' answered the cook.

'How!' exclaimed Cosmo. 'Did they know you were coming?'

'No.'

'Then why have they prepared dinner?'

'You forget. I am only one in this house. My presence or absence never affects the dinner.'

'Well,' thought Cosmo, snuffing the air, 'I'll let him have one good dinner before the deluge.'

.   .   .   .   .   .

'And now,' said Ninian in the study after dinner, 'you say that I must fail because I am trusting to my money.'

'I say so,' said Cosmo. 'I have an intuitive feeling—something like prophecy, perhaps—that your wealth is as unstable as your dreams, and will take to itself wings.'

'Have you no theory?'

'Not in this case; instinct, pure and simple.'

'But surely you could make a theory. I am in the humour to be amused. And that reminds me that you haven't your fool's dress on, Master Cosmo; and that you ran away from Tullibolton, Master Cosmo; and I shall require to punish you, Master Cosmo, but I bear you no ill-will, remember. I can whip you when {you change your dress. Come upstairs.'

'I will not change my dress, and you shall not whip me.'

'Now, what an ass you are! You know perfectly well that you will have to do just as I like.'

'Never again, Master Jamieson. You have over-shot yourself, Master Jamieson; you are bought and sold, Master Jamieson. I see an ominous missive on your desk, Master Jamieson ; you had better read it.'

From several unopened letters Cosmo chose one in a large blue envelope with the London postmark and handed it to Ninian, who took it in a dazed way. Staring blankly at Cosmo he opened the envelope, and then with a shiver turned his eyes on the letter. After reading it twice he staggered from the room, crushing the letter with both hands. In a few minutes he returned, followed by the pretty maid-servant with a decanter of the 'Dunmyatt Whisky' and two horns. Having filled the horns she withdrew. Ninian was very white, but he now walked with a firm step. He took from his desk a roll of manuscript, and before sitting down handed one of the horns to Cosmo, who noticed for the first time a large ring with a bloodstone on the Provost's left hand.

'My very good friend,' said Ninian, 'let us pledge each other.'

He emptied his horn, but Cosmo drank only a little of his.

'My money and my dreams have melted away,' said Ninian. 'My imagination, like a bird plunged suddenly into a dungeon, dashes blindly against

stony blackness.   It is hard—it is terrible.   Do
you not think it possible?   Do you believe that if
I had spent my whole capital, my hundred and fifty
thousand, in bribing the garrison that I couldn't
have reigned in Stirling for one day?   You neither
know me nor the power of money if you think so.
All gone—all gone!   My father left it safe; why
wasn't I content?   Cosmo, keep clear of Asiatic
coal and gold.'

'You forget.   I have an annuity.'

'An annuity: ay, you are wise.   Perhaps you
think of writing my life, Cosmo.   I charge you not
to do so.   If you speak of me at all, say that I had
the faults of the Stuarts, but that I knew it and
strove to conquer them.   Should any one in your
hearing talk of me as mad, say to him that I was
not mad, but that after reading two thousand novels
I learnt who I was: that, I think, will explain my
mistakes.   This is my pedigree,' he said with a faint
smile, shaking out the manuscript which he held in
his hand.   'It is useless now, as I have no heir.'

He glanced through the pages, and then lighting
them with a match burnt them to ashes.

'You will go to-morrow to Tullibolton and tell
Marjory that I loved her.'

When he had said that Ninian raised his left

hand to his mouth. Cosmo heard a slight click
and sprang towards him. At the same time wheels
sounded on the gravel outside. Ninian's hand fell,
and something dropped lightly on the floor.

'Who can it be?' he said hoarsely.

He stood listening; and Cosmo watched him
silently until the footman came.

'A lady to see you, sir,' he said.

'Who is it?'

'She won't give her name.'

Ninian rushed to the drawing-room and found
Marjory Morton.

'I did not think you would be at home. I had
no intention of seeing you when I called,' she
said.

She was standing in the centre of the room, one
hand clutching the other convulsively. Her hair
had lost its curl and hung in tangles; her lips were
white and thin, and the roundness seemed gone from
her cheeks; but her eyes shone. Ninian, looking
in her face, touched her on the shoulder and stepped
back.

'I hardly know why I am here,' she continued.
'The servant said you were at home and I came in.
I wanted to leave something, and asked, without
thinking, when you would be home, and the

servant said you were in.' Oh! I have brought you some money I don't need.'

She took some money from her pocket and laid it on a table with an inlaid marble top. In doing so her eyes caught a crack in one of the pieces, and she traced it carefully with her finger-nail.

'Good-bye,' she said, looking up.

'Why have you brought me money?' asked Ninian.

'You are bankrupt, are you not?'

'How should you know?—I am.'

'Then you must be needing money.'

'But——'

'Ask me nothing. Let me go.'

She had seized the door-handle before Ninian could stop her. When she felt his grasp on her arm she stood passively.

'Marjory,' said Ninian, with his mouth at her ear.

She turned and tried to look at him, but her eyelids fell in spite of an effort that made her tremble from head to foot.

'Marjory,' he said again.

Paler than before, and shaking, she leant against the door. Ninian gathered her up in his arms. He also shook, and stumbling into a low chair nearly

let her fall ; she felt him reeling and clasped him
instinctively.

'Marjory,' he said a third time.

Her mouth was still sealed, but she did not relax
her grasp ; her eyes were tightly closed—so tightly
that her brows were contracted.   He bent over her
and sought through her eyelids for her eyes ; he
searched her brow in a strong endeavour to fathom
her mind ; he kissed her mouth, hoping to reach her
heart—a long kiss, for she did not move until he
raised his head to look at her.   He marvelled at the
change.   Her eyes were closed but a tear hung on
each eyelid ; a deep blush had restored the form to
her cheek, and her lips had grown full and red ; her
very hair had come alive again, the gold about her
temples shone, and the tangles began to crisp.   She
opened her eyes slowly, the long lashes shook off
the teardrops, and the black living pupil filled up
the whole iris.   He felt a beam of light pass from
her eyes to his and bent to kiss her again, but she
hid her face in his breast.   Then they said the
things that lovers say.

'Did you love me at the first ?' said she.

'I loved you from the moment I saw you.   And
you ?'

'I haven't slept since I met you at midnight.'

K

'Did you really not expect to find me here?'

'Really. I wished to be some place where you had been. I wished to do something connected with you. There's fifty pounds. It's not very much, but it may help you a little. I had thirty, and aunt lent me twenty.'

'Your aunt? I thought she objected to me.'

'But aunt and I are friends now.'

'Fifty pounds,' mused Ninian, smiling. 'Dear— my dear!'

'I suppose bankrupts are very poor?'

'Sometimes.'

'Are you very poor?'

'Very.'

'I'm very poor too. I've got nothing now, and I owe aunt twenty pounds. But I'm glad I'm poor, and I'm glad you're poor. You'll never mind being king now, dear.'

'No.'

'But you'll show me the documents.'

'They are burned.'

'Burned! And were you coming to me?'

'No.'

'What were you going to do?'

'I'll tell you when we're married.'

At that moment had their ears not been throbbing

with their own blood they would have heard Cosmo
stealing from the door and muttering, 'It is this
love that spoils greatness, and eccentricity.'   He
returned to the study and picked from the floor a
small blue crystal.   Having wrapped it in a bit of
an old letter he placed it in his vest pocket.   Then
he finished his whisky and left the house un-
observed.

PART II

THE PILGRIMAGE OF STRONGSOUL AND SAUNDERS ELSHANDER

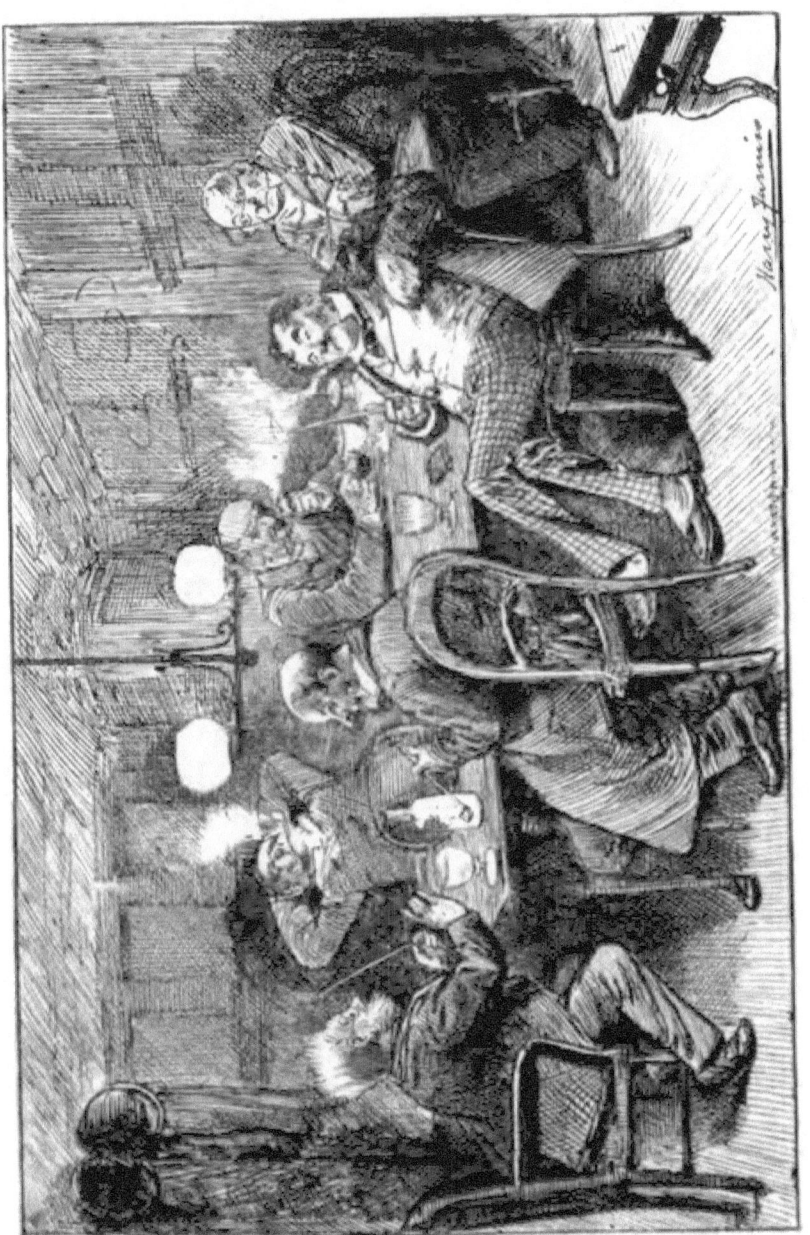

The Meeting of the Great Men.

CHAPTER I

THE GREAT MEN

IN a back room in a quiet street in Edinburgh on a December night, some ten or twelve years after Ninian's campaign, five men sat round a table smoking churchwarden pipes and drinking whisky-toddy. It was an old-fashioned room with an old-fashioned fireplace; and the fire was old-fashioned too, for it was wood that the Great Men burned. They had a contract with a turner, and got from him all his waste birch. What a fire it makes— clear, red, and strong—and the ash like powdery snow! Then the smell of its burning, so delicate and pungent! 'Frankincense!' Cosmo Mortimer burst out once. 'Birch-wood as far surpasses incense as a Scotch lassie surpasses the world. Gentlemen, there is an aroma'—passing his hand across the fire, and wafting the smoke to the nostrils of the Great Men—'a sweet homely smell of the mountain and

the flood in the smoke of birch——a fleeting memory
of everything high and noble, and beautiful and true,
in the life of the Scotch people and the history of
the Scotch nation.'

But Cosmo was not present on the night in
question. His armchair stood vacant at the head of
the table, and the other members of the club he had
formed waited with dull impatience for his arrival.
The wind rumbled in the chimney, and the snow,
like flights of white moths drawn to the light,
thudded softly against the window.

'Cosmo was never late before,' said a melancholy-
looking Great Man, who smoked with extreme
gravity and regularity, and moistened his lips with
whisky-toddy at every sixth puff.

'It's twenty minutes past the hour,' said the
Great Man who was secretary, looking a very large
gold watch, and speaking with the confidence of one
who knows that he is stating a fact.

'He's very late,' said a timid Great Man, hastily
snatching from those who had not yet spoken that
view of the subject.

'The very thing I was about to say,' said the
fourth Great Man, smiling triumphantly, for he knew
that he had forestalled the fifth Great Man.

What the fifth Great Man thought of saying after

his intended contribution to the conversation had
been stolen can never be known, for, while he was
still pondering a new remark, Cosmo entered the
room in a huge great-coat which stuck out very
much on one side.

They rose to receive him, and the secretary said
in the form prescribed by the rules of the club,
'The Great Men are all met,' whereupon the
melancholy Great Man who was honorary porter
locked the door and closed the shutters. Then they
resumed their seats. Cosmo, looking mysteriously
at the faces of the Great Men, took from under his
overcoat a little barrel, and placed it ceremoniously
on the table. Having divested himself of his wraps
he warmed his hands at the fire, and sank into the
president's chair.

'Fresh glasses,' he said.

The timid Great Man, who was honorary steward,
took from a cupboard six large old-fashioned rummers and set them on the table.

'The corkscrew—the large one ; a filler and a
bottle,' said the president.

The honorary steward, standing on tip-toe, un-
hooked from the wall an instrument like a twisted
dagger, and produced the other articles from the
cupboard. The bung was removed, the bottle filled,

and the rummers filled from the bottle ; it was a
quart bottle but it had to be replenished, for the six
rummers held half a gallon.

Then the president rose, rummer in hand, and the
five Great Men followed his example.

'This,' said Cosmo with emotion, 'is the "Dunmyatt Whisky." I propose the health of Mr. and
Mrs. Ninian Jamieson.'

Cosmo drank slowly about an inch of his rummer and sat down ; and the other Great Men did
likewise. They had heard of the 'Dunmyatt
Whisky,' and they knew the history of Ninian
Jamieson—Cosmo's version. Their excitement was
intense ; their curiosity boundless. Cosmo liked the
situation. He sipped his rummer twice, and held it
to his nose, inhaling the fragrance of the famous
whisky. 'There are only ten barrels left,' he sighed.
At length he spoke up briskly. 'This morning I
took a run north to Mintern, to find out how Jamieson had got on. You remember the last news we
had—his resignation of the provostship ? Well, I
called at his house, and who should be at the window
but his wife, Marjory Morton that was, Mrs. Ninian
Jamieson that is. She was, of course, very glad to
see me, and gave me at once a glass of the "Dunmyatt." We talked away brilliantly until Jamieson

came in. I shook hands with him, gentlemen, as if we had never been anything but the closest friends, and he seemed much relieved. I stayed for dinner. It was a dinner very unlike those which I had formerly eaten in that house, but it was quite good. We dined at two ; there was only one servant, and she didn't sit at the table. Everything is on a reduced scale, and more than half the house is shut up. After dinner Ninian told me how they had gone to Perth and been married by the Sheriff. They seemed quite happy ; in fact I envied Ninian, for his wife is a glorious creature, and I can't imagine how I let her slip through my fingers. When I came away he made me a present of this barrel.'

'And Thomsina ?' said the melancholy man.

'Oh! she has taken a house in Mintern, ordered half a dozen mob-caps, and is going to set up old maid.'

'Did all Jamieson's money go?' asked the secretary.

'No ; some hundreds were saved.'

'And how's he living?' asked the honorary steward in his timid hurried way, again forestalling the other two.

'That's just what I was going to ask,' said the

fourth man, taking the words out of the fifth man's
lips for the second time.

'Well, gentlemen,' said Cosmo, measuring his
words in a manner very unusual with him, 'Ninian
Jamieson may, I think, be said to be at last developing greatness.   The only means of making a liveli-
hood with which he has any practical acquaintance
is the grocer trade.   So he opened a shop in Mintern, and has a good custom although he doesn't sell
"Dunmyatt Whisky."   I think it an exceedingly
daring thing to do in the town where he had been
envied and caressed.   Yet there he is selling tea and
sugar across his counter———'

'Like an ancient Roman,' said the fifth man with
an illuminated countenance, speaking for the first
time.

'No, sir,' said Cosmo severely, 'like a modern
Scot.'

But the fifth man was not quenched.   Certain
this time that he had hit on something that had not
occurred to the others, he asked with the dignity of
a judge, 'Have they any children?'

Cosmo did not answer immediately.   He sipped
his whisky, looked dreamily at the ceiling, pushed
back his chair and then said, 'I'll tell you a
story.'

Two of the Great Men buttoned their coats, and three of them unbuttoned their vests ; they filled their pipes, drank half an inch of whisky each, and assumed various easy or uneasy postures. Then without any ·prelude Cosmo began.

CHAPTER II

COSMO MORTIMER'S STORY

ON one of the paths that wind about Dunmyatt, at four o'clock on a June morning, a little boy walked slowly, bearing a heavy burden on his back. Larks were shouting in the sky, and in and out of the clefts in the rocks gray-cowled jackdaws flew croaking and screaming. The little boy trudged wearily along, seeing and hearing nothing, his head bent forward like an old man's. With one hand he supported his burden, for the rope that tied it round his waist and shoulders had slackened. In his other hand he carried a stick of oak, which he used at every step to help him on. It was no wonder he was tired, for he had been on the road since two o'clock that morning. Still he would not give in, and he tottered along the winding sheep-path, gasping for breath, and with the sweat running down his face. He was a strong little boy; his legs were like little oak-trees. He would have gone on until he dropped had he not met another boy on the sheep-path. The other boy was much taller, and carried, rolled up under his arm, a white apron. He was a shepherd's son, apprenticed to a grocer, on his way

to open his master's shop in Tullibody, a village about two miles from Dunmyatt.

The grocer's boy said, 'Whaur are ye gaun?'

The little boy looked at him very closely and said, 'Who are you?'

'Never you mind.   Tell me whaur ye're gaun.'

'I'm going away to the west,' said the little boy.

'I see that.   But whaur tae?'

'I don't like to tell you.   If I knew who you
were I might.   Are you Obstinate?'

'Eh?' said the grocer's boy angrily.   'What dae
ye mean?'

'You can't be Pliable,' said the little boy, 'because you're too gruff; but then you seem to be
coming the wrong way.   You're not Evangelist, are
you?'

Look here, my mannie, nane o' your impidence,
or I'll heave ye owre the hill.   It strikes me ye've
been daein' what ye shouldna.   What hae ye in
that bag?'

'I wish I knew who you were,' said the little boy.

'I'm Saunders Elshander, the son o' Rab Tam-
son's shepherd.   Wha are you?'

'I'm not very sure,' said the little boy.

'No!' said Saunders, bursting into a loud laugh;
'mebbe the polis would mak' ye surer than ye're
carin' tae be.   What hae ye in that bag?'

The little boy looked at the ground and then,
raising his head, said with much gravity, 'My sins.'

'I'm thinkin' sae,' said Saunders.   'Whaur did ye
steal them?'

The little boy's eyes blazed and he grasped his stick tightly ; but he answered quietly, 'I didn't steal them. They are my sins. I am a pilgrim, and this is my burden.'

'Ye're a strange one,' said Saunders ; 'come, let's see what ye've got.'

Saunders laid hold of the rope and untied the burden. 'Losh bless me, it's a pillowslip !' he cried.

The little boy was inclined to resist, but he seemed to be in a difficulty ; so he allowed his burden to be examined. The first thing Saunders pulled out was some shavings. These he threw up in the air, and the wind caught them and blew them down the hillside. Then he pulled out a broken poker, which he pitched away. Several pieces of firewood came next. 'I've nae time tae waste,' he said, taking up the pillowslip and shaking out its contents. With a piece of the firewood he raked among them, but finding nothing of much value he kicked and tossed everything down the hillside.

'Man,' he said, 'thae's no worth stealin'.'

But the little boy had taken a book from his pocket, and was turning over its pages very eagerly.

'Ma certie !' said Saunders, 'ye're the strangest laddie I ever met in wi'. What's this ye've gotten noo ?'

L

He snatched the book, and, turning to the first page, read the title, *The Pilgrim's Progress*.

'Ay, man,' he added with a sneer, 'an' sae ye read *The Pilgrim's Progress*, dae ye?   My granny reads it.   What's it aboot?'

He turned over its pages carelessly, and then threw it away after the contents of the pillowslip, saying, 'Ye can ging after your bookie, if ye like.'

Immediately the little boy dealt him a thundering blow on the head with his oaken stick, and shouted at the same time, 'I know you now.   You are Apollyon disguised as a grocer's boy.   Come on, for I fear you not.'

He hit Saunders another rap on the head, and followed it up with a third.   Then Saunders, who, although he delighted in mischief, was not a coward, turned with a roar and wrenched the stick from the little boy's hand, but it slipped from his grasp and rolled down the hill a little way.   The two stood facing each other for several seconds, the little boy quite undaunted, and the other wondering how much damage he would have to sustain before conquering his opponent.   Determined to have the fight over at once, he put in two rapid and heavy blows on the little boy's face.   The little boy lowered his head, and butting Saunders in the stomach upset him ;

but, being unable to stop his rush, he fell upon him,
and both rolled down the hill.   The little boy was
being severely mauled when his hand touched the
stick.   He seized it, and with a great effort wriggled
himself free.   Springing to his feet he whirled the
stick round his head and brought it down with all
his might on Saunders's nose, shouting at the same
time, 'Have at you, fiend!'   He raised the stick
for another blow, but his enemy lay stunned, so
fiercely had the little fellow struck him.   With a
look of satisfaction the conqueror kicked the fallen
Saunders in the ribs, and then crawled down the hillside after his book.   He had no difficulty in finding
it, and he also succeeded in recovering a pair of shoes,
two pairs of stockings, and a jacket.   With these he
climbed up the hill again, and found Saunders leaning
on his elbow and wiping his bloody swollen face with
his grocer's apron.

'Ye wee teeger!' he groaned.   'If I get a hold
o' ye I'll murder ye.'

The little boy was very much disappointed, for he
thought he had killed him ; but he took his stick and
shouted, 'Come on, then.'

'Lay doon that rung an' come an' help me.   Is
there ony water aboot?'

The little boy laid down his stick, put his hands

in his pockets, and stared at Saunders with unaffected amazement, and so solemnly that Saunders, in spite of his wounds and bruises, burst out laughing.

'Man,' he said, 'ye mind me o' a thing ma granny says——

> ' " The gravest fish's an oyster,
>   The gravest bird's an owl ;
>   The gravest beast's an ass,
>   The gravest man's a fool." '

Here the little boy tottered and fell down as white as a ghost. The sudden excitement of the meeting with Saunders had made him forget his fatigue ; but now his long walk, his exertions in the fight, and his empty stomach—for he had eaten nothing since the previous night—overcame him utterly. He did not faint, but he was very sick and weak.

'Hech, man !' cried Saunders ; 'what's this noo ? Hae ye seen green cheese that your een reel that gait ?'

'I'm not well,' said the little boy. He put out his hand for his book, but he was unable to reach it. Saunders handed it to him, and the little boy read in it for a minute. Saunders looked on in astonishment.

When he had done reading he closed his book

and said, 'I have made a mistake; you are not Apollyon.'

'I dinna ken,' said Saunders; 'wha was he?'

'Apollyon is one of the names of the devil,' answered the little boy.

'Weel, it's the first time I've been mista'en for the de'il, though it's no the first time I've been called one.'

'Saunders Elshander,' said the little boy, rising up with the help of his stick, 'I humbly beg your pardon.'

He held out his hand, and Saunders, rising, took it and said, 'It's a' richt.'

Then they looked at each other for a minute. Then Saunders said, 'I think there's water at the foot o' the brae.'

With that he took his apron and the little boy's jacket and shoes and stockings and put them into the pillowslip. The little boy got hold of his stick and his book, and Saunders gave him his arm, and they went down the hill in a zig-zag way till they came to a little stream. There they washed themselves and drank, and Saunders took out of his pocket some bread and cheese and gave half of it to the little boy; and when the little boy had eaten it he fell fast asleep.

Now Saunders was in a difficulty. Should he go to the shop at once, or should he wait until his late enemy waked? If he were to run all the way he could not now be in time to open the shop. He felt certain also that his master would not allow him to serve customers, or even to go errands, with his swollen head and nose, for he had seen his face in a pool and had been quite scared by it. His nose seemed to have spread over his face, and his head looked like a lumpy potato. Still he felt that he ought to go and let his master know what had befallen him as soon as possible. His master would cuff him soundly; but Saunders was no coward. He shrugged his shoulders with a rueful look, however, when he thought of his father and a certain stick which stood in the chimney-corner, and of his grandmother, whose tongue was even more terrible to him than his father's stick. He looked at his companion, and was quite ashamed to see what a pair of black eyes he had given him—a little fellow, only two-thirds of his size. He felt his arms and legs, and then felt his own, and was not quite so much ashamed. The little boy's shoulders, too, were so broad, and he had such a look of strength and determination, even in his sleep, that Saunders came to the conclusion that by the time they were both men

the little boy would be much more than a match for
him.   Then his eyes wandered over the hillside, and
he saw some of the wood and things that he had
tumbled out of the pillowship, and he at once set to
work to gather as many of them as he could.   He
got together almost everything except the shavings,
and filled the pillowslip again.   He felt quite happy
when he had done this, and sat down beside the little
boy, who still slept.   He wondered very much who
this little boy could be, and what he meant by his
burden and his being on a pilgrimage ; he lay wondering and wondering until the little boy wakened,
after sleeping two hours.

The little boy looked graver than ever, and
observing that his pillowslip was packed again he
held out his hand to Saunders once more, who took
it and pressed it hard.   Then, because the sun was
strong, they went up the stream to a place where an
old thorn-tree grew, and laid themselves down in the
shadow of it.

'Now,' said the little boy, 'I shall tell you who I
am.   I am the pilgrim Strongsoul.'

'Strongsoul !' said Saunders ; 'I never heard the
name afore.'

'I never heard it till I said it just now,' said the
little boy, 'except in my dream.'

'In your dream!' echoed Saunders.

'Yes,' said Strongsoul, 'I had a dream just now. You must know, Saunders Elshander, that *The Pilgrim's Progress* is the greatest book in the world. Once you have read it you don't need, and you don't want, to read any other. All that you want to do is to become a pilgrim. I began my pilgrimage this morning, but I made a great mistake. I expected that everything would happen to me just as it happened to Christian; but when I had walked for six hours, and got on to the shoulder of Dunmyatt without Pliable or Obstinate coming after me, and without meeting Evangelist or Worldly Wiseman, I began to doubt that something was wrong. Then I met you, and I couldn't make out who you were, for there is nobody like you, Saunders Elshander, in the whole of *The Pilgrim's Progress* from beginning to end. And because things were happening so differently from what I expected, I doubted that I was wrong in thinking myself another Christian, so I told you that I wasn't very sure who I was. Then when you emptied my burden at the very beginning of my pilgrimage, I thought that you were the devil, although at first I wasn't sure that you mightn't be an angel. Then I attacked you, and when I had overcome you, and you asked me to help you, I

wondered very much, and thought it was a new
temptation of yours to get me into your clutches ;
but when I fell down beside you and you did
nothing to me, I saw that you weren't the devil ; so
I begged your pardon. And now about my dream.
Methought I saw one in shining raiment who came
to me and said, " Thy name is Strongsoul, and thy
fame and glory shall equal Greatheart's. Arise and
follow me." And I arose and followed. And the
shining one took me to the top of Dunmyatt, and
showed me afar off the smoke of a great city, and
said, " There lies the City of Destruction." And
the shining one vanished, and I awoke. Now the
meaning and interpretation of the dream is this : I
am henceforth to be called Strongsoul, and we are
to journey first of all to the City of Destruction, and
thence start for the Celestial City. Thus we cannot
expect to meet with any of the adventures which
Christian met with until we arrive at the City of
Destruction. Wherefore, arise and let us go thither.'

Saunders understood only a little of what Strongsoul told him, but he was very much impressed
with the earnest way in which he spoke, so he
thought he would take his advice about the difficulty regarding the shop. When Strongsoul heard
what Saunders had to say he advised him not to

return either to his master or his father, but to become a pilgrim like him. This proposal staggered Saunders, and he had objections to urge against it. First of all he asked if it wouldn't be wrong.

Strongsoul answered him out of his book, and showed him a picture in which Evangelist gave Christian a parchment-roll, wherein was written, 'Flee from the wrath to come.'

'Ay,' said Saunders, 'my granny's wrath's gey ill tae bear. But we would be sure tae be ta'en up on the road and sent hame.'

'We might,' said Strongsoul. 'There is no adventure of that kind in the book ; but it might happen to us.'

'What would ye dae then?' asked Saunders.

'We might escape from the enemy before they brought us back. If we didn't, we would just have to start again when we were free.'

Saunders began to be overpowered by Strong-soul's inability to conceive of any other course than the undertaking of this pilgrimage at every hazard. Still he had an argument left, and he thought it a strong one.

'Hoo are we tae live on the road?' he asked.

Strongsoul again answered him out of his book. He showed him a picture of the Palace Beautiful, and read him the passage where the porter says that it was built 'for the relief and security of the pilgrims.' He added, 'You may be sure, Saunders, that if it takes more than a day to get to the City of Destruction, some lodging or arbour will be provided for us.'

Saunders liked the idea of a roving life, and had more than once thought of running away to sea, so he agreed to accompany Strongsoul on his pilgrimage. They found a sheep-path which led south-east, the direction, Strongsoul said, of the City of Destruction, and they followed it for a while, talking about their pilgrimage, and of other pilgrims who had had adventures with giants, and in the Enchanted Ground, and in the Land of Beulah.

CHAPTER III

COSMO MORTIMER'S STORY—*Continued*

AFTER an hour's journey they found that the sheep-path ceased to go in the direction of the City of Destruction, so they went down to the stream again to rest and to determine how they should proceed. They would have come to a decision about the way much more easily if they had climbed a hill instead of going down into a valley, but they were both thirsty and hungry, and Strong-soul expected to find an arbour beside the water where they could refresh themselves with fruit, and receive some miraculous indication of the way they should take. Saunders, who did not understand pilgrimages so well as Strongsoul, took out of his pocket as they came near the stream a loop of twisted horse-hair, which he told Strongsoul was a girn. He, too, was concerned about his hunger, but he had an idea of his own as to the likeliest way of satisfying it.

Strongsoul did not know what a girn was,
because he had not mingled much with other boys,
and so Saunders told him it was for catching trout.
Strongsoul wondered how fish could be caught with
a little running-noose of horse-hair, and was inclined
to think that his companion was making fun of him.
Saunders was glad to find that he knew about something better than Strongsoul, and he became very
important indeed, and had a great rubbing and
sorting of his girn, and quoted a saying of his grandmother's that 'fools an' bairns shouldna see things
half done.'

Strongsoul paid no heed to him, but began to
look about for an arbour. Now it chanced that
there was a little den by the bank of the stream just
where they descended. It was enclosed by hazels
and thorns, and there was a mossy stone in the
centre of it like a table, and the turf about it was
thick and green and sprinkled with daisies. The
stream paused for a little at this place in a broad
and deep pool ; then it dived over some rocks, and
hurried away as if to make up for the time it had
spent beside the den ; and it sang as it went. There
were no fruit-trees in the den, but Strongsoul was
mightily pleased with it, and pointed out all its
beauties to Saunders with much pride. Saunders

admired everything, especially the pool, and he
laughed with delight when he saw that there were
trout in it.   He cut a hazel wand, and tied his girn to
the slim end of it with horse-hair, and was just
beginning to fish when the humble attention which
Strongsoul paid him suggested the idea of exhibiting
more of his superiority.   He laid his hazel wand on
the turf, and sitting down on the mossy stone put
one leg over the other and began to nurse his knee.
He did not know how to start the subject which he
wanted to talk about ; besides, it was necessary to
find out whether he had more acquaintance with it
than Strongsoul.   He puckered his brows, and was
afraid he would have to give it up for the time
being when he suddenly saw how to work up to his
point.

' Hoo heavy are ye ? ' he asked.

' I don't know,' said Strongsoul.

' Man, dae ye no ken that !   I'm eight stane.'

Strongsoul was not interested, but Saunders went
on.

' An' eight stane's a hunner an' twal' pun'.'

Strongsoul took out his book and began to read.
This Saunders regarded as a sign that he knew
nothing about Weights and Measures ; therefore,
without more delay, he launched into *Avoirdupois*

Weight, going straight through it at a breathless rate. Then he rushed through *Measure of Capacity*, ending up with the irregular measures, which he enunciated slowly and with much emphasis. He knew this to be a feat, as there had been only two other boys besides himself in school with him able to do so correctly at a moment's notice.

Strongsoul continued to read his book as if there had been nobody present but himself. Saunders perceived now, clearly, that he was master here, for he could not imagine any boy who knew Weights and Measures remaining for one second under the supposition of ignorance of such a subject—a subject which had been to him the most difficult he had mastered.

'Dae ye ken *Lineal Measure?*' he asked, his eyes blazing with triumph.

Strongsoul said nothing.

'Man, it's quite easy. I learned it in a week, an' I never got mair nor sax palmies for mistakes in't ; an' Geordie Simpson, him that got the prize for coontin', aince got twelve for't in one day.'

Then Saunders went through *Lineal Measure* gloriously.

'I say,' he cried breathlessly, 'dae ye ken the Multiplication Table? Dae ye ken thirteen times?'

At last Strongsoul laid down his book, and, coming up to him, stood with his hands behind his back and gazed at him sternly.

'Saunders Elshander,' he said, 'it seems to me that you would be better employed at one of the booths in Vanity Fair, or in the school of Mr. Gripeman, in Lovegain, which is a market-town in the county of Coveting, in the north, than in going on pilgrimage. This is carnal knowledge, and you must never speak of Weights and Measures to me again. Such talk might do in the company of Mr. Byends, Mr. Hold-the-World, Mr. Moneylove, and Mr. Saveall, but it is not becoming in true pilgrims. I never knew much of this carnal knowledge, and I have forgotten all I knew. You must do the same, or there is no use your going on pilgrimage.'

'But hoo can I forget what was thrashed intae me?'

'Well, Saunders, I don't know, but if you go on with your fishing I'll think about it.'

'A' richt,' said Saunders.

He was a little crestfallen, but he felt confident that his fishing would create a sensation, so he applied himself to it with all the skill he had. Strongsoul lay down on the bank and watched him, thinking how he was to make Saunders forget his

Weights and Measures ; but he soon ceased to do so in the excitement of the fishing.

Saunders knew perfectly well what he was about. The first thing he did was to look up and down the pool to see if there were any trout basking in the sun. At length he caught sight of one snoozing on a flat brown stone. He measured with his eye the distance of the trout from the bank, and laid the girn upon the water about three feet in front of the trout's head. Very gently he lowered the point of his wand into the water, sloping it towards the trout, until the girn was exactly opposite the trout's nose. The trout moved its fins and shifted its position about an inch. Saunders followed the motion with his girn.

I don't know whether he or Strongsoul was more excited. If he failed to catch this trout at once it would be a terrible downcome, no matter how many more he might catch afterwards. His heart beat, and his eye glared as if his life depended on what he was about. Strongsoul was excited because he perceived now how the girn was to be used. When it occurred to him he rejected the idea as absurd. How could anybody pass a running-noose over a trout's head, and pulling it back behind the gills whip the trout out of the water !

Saunders moved the girn up and down slowly until it was only two inches from the trout. Now was the critical moment! He was on his knees. He clenched his teeth, and clutched the turf with his left hand. With a backward motion of the right the noose was over the trout's head, as cleanly as if the trout had sailed into it. A pause, an upward jerk, and a sweep to the left landed the trout on the turf, wriggling at the end of the hazel wand.

'Hurrah!' cried Strongsoul, laughing with delight.

Saunders undid the noose, and putting his thumb into the trout's mouth broke its neck.

'How heavy do you think it is?' asked Strongsoul.

'Near quarter a pun',' said Saunders, stepping back to the pool.

Another trout had come out from its hole to see what had disturbed the water. It was about as big as the one just caught, and lay very finely; but as Saunders dropped his girn on the water it slipped off the stone and moved slowly in below another one. With the butt-end of his wand Saunders poked it out, when it rushed in below the opposite bank. Saunders quickly took off his boots and stockings and stepped into the pool. He was afraid

to thrust his wand into the bank lest he should
make the water muddy, so he went round to the
trout's hole and waited. In a minute it popped out
its nose and snuffed the water. It seemed to be of
opinion that the coast was clear, for it moved away
to the middle of the pool and lay down on the
gravel to think. It was trying to account for the
absence of its friend, the trout which Saunders had
caught. Its cold brain had even got the length of
connecting the knock in the ribs it had itself received
with the disappearance of the other trout when it
saw a black circle in the water about three inches
from it. It was a harmless-looking circle, so the
trout thought it had better swim through it. One
motion of his fins and the circle was behind it, and
it felt quite safe.

But it was not quite safe. The whole of its tail
and an inch of its body were still within the girn.
Saunders was in a terrible state. The perspiration
ran down his face, and it was only by a great effort
that he kept his wand steady. He had never seen
it done before, he had never even heard of its being
attempted, but it seemed to him quite possible now
to girn a trout by the tail. It was a big trout, and
the tail looked strong enough to hold the noose.
He hesitated, until he saw how stupid he was, with

a trout in his girn, not to try to land him, no matter by which end. Just as he jerked the girn the trout rose to a fly. This was the very best thing that could have happened, for the noose was so tightened by the double motion of the jerk and of the rising of the trout that Saunders landed him with the greatest ease.

Now this was exceedingly good girning, two trout in ten minutes, as Saunders very well knew. Still he took his success as a matter of course ; and when Strongsoul exclaimed about his having caught the second fish by the tail he simply said, ' Ay, oh ay !' as if it were quite an ordinary thing to do. But he did not girn any more at that time, as he had no wish to risk his reputation.

' Help me tae mak' a fire,' he said, 'an' we'll cook thae troot.'

Strongsoul wished to distinguish himself in practical matters too, so he undid the pillowslip and arranged some of the sticks for the fire. He then went to a wire-fence that crossed the stream at a little distance from the den. One of the lower wires was quite slack, and from it he twisted a piece about two yards long. While he was doing this he looked out of the corner of his eye to see what impression he was making on Saunders, and he was greatly

delighted to find that Saunders watched him twisting
the wire as closely as he had watched Saunders
girning the trout.

One thing annoyed Strongsoul very much. He
had no matches. Saunders evidently had some, or
he would not have been so ready to make a fire.
Everybody knows the extraordinary satisfaction there
is in making a blaze, especially in the open air, and
this glory was to be added to that already won by
Saunders with the girn. But Strongsoul, good
pilgrim though he was, tried to dim the lustre of it.

'Why don't you light the fire?' he asked.

'I thocht ye were gaun' tae dae't wi' that wire,'
said Saunders.

'Oh no!' said Strongsoul. 'This is for a very
much more important thing.'

'What is't for?'

'Light the fire and you'll see.'

Saunders felt that the deference due to him as
the possessor of matches had been withheld, and he
thought that Strongsoul took a mean advantage in
pretending—for he knew it was pretence—such in-
difference. However he lit the fire quietly, saying, as
he applied the match, 'They're gey big fish, thae twa.'

Strongsoul said nothing, but began to shape the
wire into something.

'It's no everybody that can girn,' said Saunders.

Still Strongsoul made no reply, and went on shaping the wire. It took him some time, for the wire was not easily bent, but with the help of his feet and a stone he succeeded in making it look something like a gridiron. He didn't look at Saunders when he was done, but placed his gridiron on the fire and was about to lay the fish on it.

.'Hold on, man!' cried Saunders. 'They're no guttit.'

Each boy pulled out a knife and seized a fish. Then each waited for the other to begin. Now Saunders knew how to clean a fish and Strongsoul did not. Strongsoul was quite prepared to clean a fish with any one who knew no more about it than he, but he had no intention of competing with an expert. He saw in Saunders's face that this was a thing he could do, so he shut up his knife and laid down the fish. The fire was needing some attention, and while Saunders took charge of the fish he built and blew it up until it glowed clear and strong.

The fish were soon cooked. Saunders produced the remainder of the bread and cheese, and as they were both hungry in a short time there was nothing left except the white bones of the trout.

After they had washed their hands and faces

Strongsoul took out his book and began to read
to Saunders. He read him the great fight with
Apollyon in the Valley of Humiliation, which
Saunders liked very much. But when Strongsoul
came to the Valley of the Shadow of Death he bade
him stop because he was frightened. Strongsoul
told him it was very stupid of him to be frightened,
and that he would come to like it in time. Although
he said this he was secretly glad to think that he
was braver than Saunders, and to make Saunders
sensible of the fact he read the whole of the Valley
of the Shadow of Death over to himself very slowly.
He read aloud again when he came to the meeting
of Christian and Faithful, and then he laid down his
book and said, ' I know now how to make you forget
your Weights and Measures, Saunders.'

' Dae ye? Man, I'll be obleeged tae ye.'

Saunders was in earnest. He was anxious to
forget even that which had been his chief glory,
because the hillside and the wind and the blue sky
began to fill him with the spirit of the pilgrim.
Weights and Measures reminded him of the school
and of the shop, and now he was to be the companion of the lark and of the flowers, and of Strongsoul, therefore he wanted to have his Weights and
Measures driven out of him.

'Yes,' said Strongsoul. 'You must change your name. Since the shining one changed my name everything that happened before is like a bad dream. How would you like to be called Faithful?'

'Him that met Christian?'

'Yes.'

'I dinna ken. Tell me mair aboot him.'

'I think he was the greatest of the pilgrims, because he suffered the most.'

'What did he suffer?'

'I'll read you about it.'

Then Strongsoul read from his book how they scourged Faithful, and buffeted him, and lanced his flesh with knives, and stoned him with stones, and pricked him with swords, and burned him to ashes at the stake.

'Dae folk dae thae things tae pilgrims noo?' asked Saunders.

'Well,' said Strongsoul, 'when Christiana, Christian's wife, with Greatheart and her family came to Vanity Fair some years after Faithful was burned, they found the people much more moderate. But then it's a very long time since that. I shouldn't wonder if they turn out to be worse than ever; we'll see when we get there.'

'An' if I was calling myself Faithfu' would they
burn me, think ye?'

'Well—they might.'

'Ay, man.'

Saunders thought for a little, and Strongsoul
watched him over the top of his book. At last he
said, 'I think ye're richt aboot changin' my name.
It would help tae change my inside. But there's
nae use garrin' things that'll grow. Noo ye tell't
me some ghaist or ither changed your name in a
dream, an' I'm thinkin' that's the richt way for
pilgrims tae get their names changed. Sae I'll wait
till a ghaist comes tae me, an' I'll gie ye my word
that I'll no think o' Weights an' Measures ony mair
than I can help, an' I'll ne'er speak o' them ava'.
Wull that dae ye?'

'That'll do,' said Strongsoul. 'Now we must go
on. We have spent too much time here already.'

Saunders shouldered the pillowslip, and they
began to climb the hill to see which way they
should go. When they got to the top of the hill all
that they saw was a valley with a higher hill on the
other side, and Saunders began to be discouraged.
But Strongsoul said, 'Let us go down into the valley
and walk along it, for I think it leads south-east,
where lies the City of Destruction.'

It was a little after noon and the sun was strong. There had been several weeks of dry weather, and as the hillside on which they were lay much exposed, the grass was burned up and very slippery. Strongsoul began to think of the way down to the Valley of Humiliation, and of the slip or two which Christian caught there.   He was therefore very wary, and taking a zigzag course moved down sideways.   But Saunders, who was accustomed to slippery hills, dug his heels firmly into the ground, took the pillowslip in both hands, and swinging it round his head sent it flying almost to the foot of the hill.   Strongsoul stood still in amazement.   Then Saunders sat down on his hunkers, clasped his knees, and with a shout slid smoothly and quickly after the pillowslip.   When he reached it he flung it to the bottom, and slid the rest of the way as he had done before.

Strongsoul considered for a second or two, and remembering that, as they had not started from the City of Destruction, their adventures and methods of going down hills did not need to be the same as those of Christian, he also got down on his hunkers. But he had no experience in the art of sliding on sun-burnt hills, so he tumbled head over heels once or twice, and rolled and stumbled and ran and jumped down to the bottom, shaking all his bones and getting several bad bruises. Saunders was sorry for him; but Strongsoul laughed and said he liked it, and Saunders respected him very much.

By this time they were hungry again, and they had no food of any kind. Saunders looked wistfully at Strongsoul once or twice, and then he asked him if there was any chance of their coming to a place provided for the refreshment of pilgrims. Strongsoul said he couldn't answer for the way in the meantime, as there was no account in his book of any journey except that from the City of Destruction. Just as he said this he spied a house at the top of the valley. He pointed it out to Saunders and told him, because he believed it, that that was a place where they could rest and refresh themselves. So they dusted with their bonnets each other's jackets and marched boldly up to the house.

The house at the top of the valley was inhabited by a small sheep-farmer. There was nobody at home when the pilgrims called except the sheep-farmer's wife. She had been married only three months, and did not know very much about life in the hills. Strongsoul knocked at the door, and the goodwife, who was a very pleasant-looking young woman, came running to open it. She was rather

astonished to find at that time two boys who were
strangers to her. Sometimes beggars passed through
the valley in the afternoon, but she had never before
had unexpected visitors so early in the day.

'Weel, laddies,' she said, 'what can I dae for
ye?'

She spoke sweetly and seemed glad to see
them, although she looked curiously at Strongsoul's blackened eyes and Saunders's swollen head.

Strongsoul answered her very courageously.

'We are pilgrims, ma'am, and we are going by
the direction of an angel to the City of Destruction.
We have need of rest and refreshment.'

The sheep-farmer's wife took a step back and
looked from one to the other. 'An' what kin' o'
refreshment would ye be wantin'?' she asked slowly.

'Scones and milk,' Saunders whispered to Strongsoul. But the goodwife heard him and burst out
laughing. 'Come in, laddies,' she said. 'Come in.'

She took them into a parlour fragrant with wood-
roof, and made them sit down on an old-fashioned
sofa at one end of it, while she sat down in an old-
fashioned armchair at the other.

'Ah-hey!' she said. 'An' sae ye're pilgrims, are
ye? Ye'll hae heard o' Christian an' Hopefu' an'
Mr. Ready-tae-halt?'

'Yes, ma'am,' said Strongsoul, with his heart in his mouth.

'An' hoo lang hae ye been on the road?'

'Since daybreak.'

'An' hae ye had naethin' tae eat sin' ye startit?'

'Oh yes, ma'am! We've had some bread and cheese and trout,' said Strongsoul. 'But we're hungry again.'

'Weel,' said the goodwife, 'bide a wee, and I'll gie ye your denner.'

Before she left the room she took from a bookshelf which hung above a chest of drawers a thick volume bound in half-calf.

'Hae ye ever seen this?' she asked, handing the book to Strongsoul.

'No,' said Strongsoul, trembling with delight as he turned over the pages.

'Ye can tak' a look at it then,' said the goodwife, 'till denner's ready.' And she left the room.

Saunders sat up close to Strongsoul and they laid the book between their knees. It was a large edition of *The Pilgrim's Progress* with a picture on every third page. They looked through it all, and Strongsoul explained the pictures to Saunders. When they had finished it they were both filled with a burning desire to get to the City of Destruction at once in order to begin their journey properly, so that they were very glad when the goodwife came and told them that dinner was ready.

She took them to the kitchen and gave them some broth and meat and potatoes, and a biscuit with jam on it and a cup of milk. Strongsoul thanked her, and Saunders said his 'denner mindit him o' a thing his granny used tae say, "It's guid tae hae oor cog oot whan it rains kail."'

'An' wha may your granny be?' said the goodwife.

But Saunders was just as pawky as she, for he said, 'She's a gey droll auld body, an' awfu' for mindin' her ain biznis—an' ither folk's tae,' he added under his breath.

The goodwife heard him and laughed, and said, 'A'tweel, laddies, it's no me that'll spoil your bit splore. I wish the gudeman had been here, for he was a gey through'ther lad himsel'.'

'But, ma'am, we are not through'ther,' said Strongsoul eagerly. 'We are pilgrims, and we would sooner cut off our right hands than do anything wrong.'

'Weel, weel, laddies, I believe ye,' said the goodwife kindly. 'I ken what it is tae want a bit

freedom. I once stayed oot a' nicht mysel' whan I
was a lassie, an' a gey sair skelpin' I got for't.'

'Come with us,' said Strongsoul, who liked the
appearance of the goodwife, and felt himself very
much drawn to her. 'Come with us. I will lead
you to the City of Destruction.'

At this the goodwife laughed louder than she had
yet done, but Strongsoul was not abashed.

'Saunders and I will help you through the Slough
of Despond,' he said, 'and past the lions and the
giants, and across the dark river to the Celestial
City.'

The goodwife stopped laughing, and the tears
came into her eyes. She took Strongsoul to her
bosom and kissed him tenderly, and said something
which Strongsoul could not perfectly understand
about having a little pilgrim of her own soon to help
her to heaven. Saunders turned his back on them
and blushed to the wall, but the goodwife clapped
him on the head and said he was a fine laddie.
Then she put some scones and oat-cakes and cheese
into the pillowslip. Besides that she gave Strongsoul a sixpence, and bade them both 'Gae hame
afore it was owre late,' having told them how to get
out of the hills to the highway.

CHAPTER IV

COSMO MORTIMER'S STORY—*Continued*

WHEN they came to the highway they began to be very downcast. The road was straight with hedges on either side, and they could see very far before them. That was the cause of their dolefulness. They had been wandering about among the hills for hours with the pleasant din of the stream, and the grasshoppers, and the bees, and the larks resounding in their ears ; with the soft turf under their feet, and paths that wound in and out and up and down, now at the water's edge, now on the brow of the hill, now among heather, now among fern. It was no wonder that the hard-beaten highway made them miserable. It stretched away for a mile in front of them thick with white dust that little puffs of wind blew in their eyes. They could see nothing on the right hand or on the left except high thorn hedges whose once glossy leaves were dry and powdered. They still

N

heard the larks singing, and sometimes a bee
twanged across the road, but these sounds made
them only regret the more the delightful paths
among the hills.

At length Saunders, who was carrying the pillowslip, could endure it no longer.   He threw down his
burden on the road and said, ' There's your sins, and
here's the last o' me,' and turned his back on Strongsoul and began to walk away.   Strongsoul ran after
him and caught him by the arm and stopped him,
and said, ' Come back, Saunders, come back.'

There was something so sweet and gentle in
Strongsoul's face as he said this that Saunders made
no resistance, and went back to where the pillowslip
lay.

' These aren't my sins, Saunders,' said Strongsoul,
picking up the pillowslip and slinging it over his
shoulder.   ' We will get our burdens when we come
to the City of Destruction.'

' What way did you call them your sins, then ? '
asked Saunders.

' Because I thought I ought to have sins just as
Christian had, and I had nothing else to make up a
burden with except these things.   I thought it didn't
matter very much what they were as long as the
burden was heavy enough.'

'Then what for dae ye lug it alang wi' ye noo?'

'Because it'll teach us how to carry burdens, and we will be better able to bear our sins when they are given to us.'

'Weel, as I said whan I first saw ye, ye're a strange one. Mebbe ye'll tell me what for ye keep trailin' through a' this stour whan we micht be trampin' the hills.'

'Because I think this must be like the narrow way, which Goodwill will show us when we have arrived at the little wicket-gate; and so we'd better get accustomed to it. Come on.'

Saunders made no answer, but started again with Strongsoul. They walked on for half an hour, neither saying anything. Then Saunders took the pillowslip from Strongsoul, and Strongsoul slipped his arm into Saunders's, and they walked along very happily in spite of the dusty road.

They had not gone far in this friendly way when they saw some one coming toward them in very ragged attire. He had a thick stick in his hand and a wallet on his back. His face was unwashed, and his beard was long and matted, and so was his hair. At the sight of this man Strongsoul began to quake, not with fear, but with the hope of an adventure. He whispered to Saunders that this looked like a

giant, and bade him be of good cheer, for he would
fight the giant and overcome him.

Now this was an ill-enough-looking man; and
when he came near the pilgrims he wondered a
little who they could be and what they were about,
but he had no intention of doing them any harm.
He was walking very fast, like one who had some
important business awaiting him; and he would
certainly have passed the pilgrims had Strongsoul
not stepped in front of him and said, 'I know thee.
Thou art giant Grislybeard, and thou hast slain
many pilgrims whom thou hast dragged out of the
king's highway; but now I will avenge their blood
upon thee. Wherefore, come on.'

With that Strongsoul lifted his stick and prepared
himself to fight, expecting the giant to do the same.
But the giant had no intention of fighting.

'Ha, ha!' he sneered. 'Get out of the way.'
And he kicked Strongsoul so that he fell and
bruised his head.

When Saunders saw Strongsoul down, although
he had little stomach for the fight and could not
understand why his companion should be so rash,
yet he plucked up courage, and swinging the pillowslip in the air made it twist round the neck of the
giant. With a pull he brought him down on his back,

saying, 'Here's a new kin' o' girnin'.' Strongsoul was on his legs again and, seeing the giant down, was about to strike him on the head when he remembered that Greatheart had never taken any advantages of the giants he had killed; so he paused until Grislybeard should rise.

The giant got up, roaring, and straightway seized

on Saunders and began to belabour him with his stick in such a savage manner that Saunders danced and shrieked with pain. But Strongsoul smote the giant a blow on the back of the head with his oaken staff. 'Coward!' he cried, 'fight with one who is armed, and leave the helpless alone.' Then the giant turned on Strongsoul with an oath and aimed

a blow at his face. Strongsoul slipped out of the
way, and put in another blow on the giant's head
which made him leap with rage and pain. He
rushed at Strongsoul and would have felled him
had not Saunders, who saw the peril of his friend
and who was now heart and soul in the fight, caught
hold of the giant's leg and tripped him up. He
rose at once, with tears of rage in his voice and
eyes at being molested and foiled by two boys. He
was no sooner on his feet, however, than Saunders,
who had got behind him, swung the pillowslip round
his neck and brought him to the ground again. In
this fall the giant's head was cut.

Afraid that he might receive some more hurt by
being taken unawares Grislybeard crawled to the
hedge before getting up, in order to be protected
from attacks with the pillowslip and to have a
position of some security from which to treat with
his enemies. The moment he was on his feet he
addressed the two pilgrims by exceedingly foul
names, and said, ' What is it you want at all ? '

' Nothing but your life will satisfy us,' said
Strongsoul.

At this the giant grew pale, thinking that the
boys were mad, and knowing how strong and
resolute madness can make even the weakest.

'Come,' said Strongsoul, 'let us fall to it again.'

The giant put up his stick to defend himself but did not leave the hedge. Strongsoul dealt a blow at him which he caught on his stick ; but the blow was very fierce, and Strongsoul's stick slipped up the giant's and struck his knuckles, bringing the blood.

Here the fight was brought to a sudden end ; for at the very moment that Strongsoul was launching another blow at Grislybeard, he himself received a stroke behind the ear and fell in a dead faint. The giant's wife, unnoticed by any of the combatants, had arrived on the scene, and she it was who had knocked Strongsoul down. There was no love lost between the giant and his wife, and they often mauled each other, but neither would allow the interference of a third party. They were so little in love that when they were on a journey they always kept about a quarter of a mile apart in order that they might not be annoyed by the sight of each other ; and that is how Mrs. Grislybeard arrived in time to save her husband.

Seeing Strongsoul no longer able to fight the giant struck Saunders across the knees and brought him down to the ground too. Then his wife helped him to bind the wound on his head, while they consulted what they should do with the defeated pilgrims.

The giantess said, 'We can't leave them here. They could describe us, and then where would we be?'

'That's true,' said the giant.

'Well, what are you going to do?' said his wife testily. 'Somebody may come along at any moment.'

'We must take them with us.'

'Must we! How?'

'Drive them before us.'

'It'll be a stiff job. We can't go along the road.'

'No; we must get off it at once. There's a break in the hedge. You go through, and I'll shove the boy after you.'

The giant's wife pushed through the hedge, and the giant lifted Strongsoul and handed him to her. Then he poked Saunders in the ribs with his stick and said, 'Get up.'

Saunders got up as well as he could with many a groan, for his knees were very sore.

'Take your bolster,' said the giant, 'and get through there.'

The opening in the hedge was pretty wide and Saunders got through well enough. Then the giant followed, and taking Strongsoul from his wife started for the hills. Mrs. Grislybeard told Saunders to follow her husband, and she brought up the rear. It was a field of turnips in which they were walking, and Saunders stumbled once or twice, but each time the giantess rapped him over the head with her stick. This made him more careful. and he managed to walk, in spite of his sore knees, without falling. He was crying to himself, however, and wished he had never seen Strongsoul.

There was a belt of trees between the turnip-field and the hills, and in it they halted. The giant forced some spirits down Strongsoul's throat, which revived him, and he opened his eyes, and sat up on the blaeberry bush where the giant had laid him. The giant and giantess also took some spirits. Then they put the pilgrims between them and resumed their journey. It was very difficult for Saunders and Strongsoul to keep up with their captors, but if either of them halted or stumbled the giantess rapped him over the head with her stick ; and as Strongsoul was too weak to fight, and had, moreover, lost his weapon, he followed the example of Saunders, and did what he could by taking heed of his steps to avoid the knocks on the head.

After they had journeyed for an hour and a half up a steep glen they rested again at a place where two streams met. The giant and giantess took some more of their cordial, and then the giantess said, 'What made you quarrel with these two boys?'

Grislybeard told his wife how the fight had begun, and that nothing had ever astonished him more in his life. Mrs. Grislybeard was astonished too, and looked at the boys, especially Strongsoul, very savagely. Strongsoul stared back. Although he managed to look at her as long as she looked at him he shuddered to the marrow of his bones at the expression of her eyes. She had once been a handsome woman, but her hair was of a dirty gray now; her brow was rough; and her face looked as if it would crumble away on the slightest touch like soft sandstone that has long been exposed to the weather. Her eyes were very ugly, and were capable of expressing only two things—greed and malignity. As a rule they had no expression at all. The malicious gleam in them as they turned from Strongsoul to the giant set Strongsoul thinking. He remembered Giant Slaygood, who was of the nature of flesh-eaters, and a cold chill ran down his back. Grislybeard and his wife might well be eaters of human flesh : the worst of cannibals could not appear more repulsive than they did. Strongsoul was puzzling his brains how Saunders and he might escape from their clutches when their captors rose, and placing the pilgrims between them started up the steeper and rockier of the two glens in the gusset of which they had been resting. The difficulty of the way took up all the attention of the pilgrims. Their heads were aching from the raps of the giantess's stick, and their feet were sore with stumbling along the rocky bed of the half-dry stream. A quarter of an hour more of this rough walking completely exhausted Strongsoul, and he fell down among the rocks unable to move a step farther. He pressed both hands on his head to save it as much as possible from the giantess's stick, and shut his eyes and clenched his teeth that he might bear the pain without crying out. But this time the giantess did not rap him on the head. Opening his eyes he saw that they were at the foot of a precipitous rock of about fifty feet high. Saunders was standing close beside him, and the giantess sat on a stone keeping guard. At first he failed to see Grislybeard, but looking about him more attentively he perceived that the rock was cleft from top to bottom, and that the giant was standing at the foot of this opening.

Grislybeard put his little finger in his mouth and whistled shrilly ; then he nodded his head ten times as if he were counting, and whistled again ; then he counted twenty in the same way, and whistled a third time. A few seconds after three whistles in rapid succession echoed down the cleft, and the giant stepped into it. In a little he reappeared and beckoned them. Strongsoul struggled to his feet and took the arm of Saunders, who was crying bitterly. The giantess pushed them on to her husband, and he lifted Saunders into a cage that was hanging inside the cleft. Viewed from the glen this cleft was only three feet across, but it opened out to six feet within the rock, and stretched away back, sometimes narrower, sometimes wider, until it was lost in darkness.

The giant stepped into the cage after Saunders, whistled once more, and they began to ascend. Strongsoul looked up and saw about the middle of the left wall the heads of two men vanishing and appearing as they worked the windlass by which the cage was being hoisted. Here, then, the giant had his cave. Once up there it would be impossible to get away. Unless he managed to escape before the cage came down he would never have another chance.

The giantess was sitting in the cleft. Behind her the rock was level for about two feet, then it sloped steeply, how far Strongsoul could not see; but this was enough for him—he knew how to make one effort for liberty.

Slowly the cage mounted, followed by the eyes of Mrs. Grislybeard and Strongsoul. Creak, crack went the chain on the windlass, while the men who were working it could be heard puffing and grunting. The giant with his stick kept the cage from bumping on the rock, and shouted to the men to hurry up. Once Saunders looked over, but he became so sick and dizzy that he had to withdraw his head. At last the cage stopped. Gathering together all his strength Strongsoul seized the feet of the giantess, and rising up turned her, screaming, head over heels down the ravine. Strongsoul looked up, but he could see nothing save the empty cage. He heard, however, angry voices, which were so loud that they had prevented the speakers from noticing the giantess's screams. Looking over the edge of the rock on which the giantess had been sitting, Strongsoul saw her at the bottom of a steep slope of nearly twenty feet, lying on her face and huddled in a heap as if dead. Then he turned and ran up the glen.

There were steep rocks on either side for about

fifty yards.   Strongsoul could, therefore, take no
other way than between these.   He chose to go up
the glen, thinking that the giant would imagine he
had tried to return to the highway as he had come,
and would in consequence search for him down the
glen.   When the precipices ended the glen was still
very steep on both sides, and Strongsoul had to
keep to the course of the stream.   Suddenly the
way was stopped by a high wall of rock which filled
up the way from side to side—all but a narrow
passage for the water.   Strongsoul sat down, and
for the first time began to despair.   He felt like a
beast caught in a trap.   But he took out his book,
and he turned to the Valley of the Shadow of Death.
He soon found the place where Christian thought of
going back, because of the company of fiends that
were coming towards him, but changed his mind,
and crying with a loud voice 'I will walk in the
strength of the Lord God' went on triumphantly.
This Strongsoul said aloud, and putting the book in
his pocket stepped into the stream.   He looked
through the narrow way that pierced the wall of
rock and saw that it was long.   Although the
stream was very low, in this channel the water ran
deep and black and still.   Strongsoul shuddered,
for there was no other way of escape ; but he said

again, not so loud as before, and indeed his voice trembled a little, ' I will walk in the strength of the Lord God,' and stepped into the passage. The water took him up to the chin at once. When he had recovered his breath his first idea was to struggle out, but he heard the sound of voices behind him. Then he muttered under his breath, ' I will walk in the strength of the Lord God,' and took a step forward. This time the water reached his nostrils, and he had to throw back his head in order to breathe. He was very white, and yet his face was dark, and the expression of it—it would be hard to say whether that was terror-stricken or terrible. He could make out distinctly now the voice of the giant in the glen ; so he prepared himself for another step. He pushed his hands forward on either side of the passage, and was just lifting his foot when he drew back. The darkness went out of his face, for his left hand had touched a ledge under the water. In a moment he was on it ; it was nearly as broad as the length of his foot. With his back to the left wall and his hands on the right one he moved along, but he had taken only four steps when he almost fell—his left hand had missed the wall. Looking up to see the cause of this, for he had been watching the water, he saw opposite him a hole. Without a moment's hesitation he sprang into it and found himself in a large cave. The first thing he did was to take the book from his pocket and lay it down to dry; then he crouched down at the entrance of the cave to listen.

Voices approached, and he heard the giant say, 'He hasn't come this way. The others must have found him by this time.' Immediately Strongsoul heard their steps receding, and soon they died away.

He was very wet, and very hungry, and very tired. If he didn't get something to eat at once he felt as if he would die. He thought very hard for ten minutes. Then he rose and stepped on to the ledge, and walked back to the entrance of the passage. He found that the ledge went all the way, but that it was deeper at the beginning, and this was how he had missed it at first.

He ran back to the giant's cave as fast as he could, and there at the foot of the cleft, as he had hoped, lay his pillowslip. It had been overlooked in the excitement caused by his escape. He knew what a risk he ran, but he could not help taking time to glance into the ravine; and he saw that the giantess had been removed. Then he hurried back to his cave, and managed to keep his pillowslip from getting wet by fastening it round his neck.

Five minutes after he got back the giant and three of his men returned to the cave, having given up the search for Strongsoul.

The pillowslip contained a suit of clothes, which Strongsoul put on, after spreading the wet ones out on the floor of the cave to dry. He ate some of the scones and cakes and cheese which the goodwife had given him, and then he lay down to think out a plan for delivering Saunders, and fell asleep.

It was night when he awoke, and looking out of his cave he saw some stars shining deep down in the water; but there was no moon. He buckled his trousers up to his thighs, and was stepping on to the ledge to go out and explore the glen when he heard voices at the entrance of the passage. He held his breath and listened.

'This is a likely place,' came from a gruff voice, doing its best to whisper.

'Who'll go first?' said another.

'I will,' said the owner of the gruff voice, and Strongsoul heard him splash into the water.

Now it was pitch dark between the walls of rock, the only visible thing being the reflection of the stars. Strongsoul thought it possible that the cave might be found by these servants of the giant—for such he judged them to be—but he perceived a

O

chance of escaping. He put his book in his pocket, pushed his pillowslip and his clothes to the back of the cave, and stepped noiselessly on to the ledge. He went up the passage a little way and waited.

'It's pretty deep,' said the gruff voice.

'So I find,' said another.

'Are ye all in?' said the gruff voice.

'Yes,' came from other two.

'Quietly, then, and cautiously.'

The speakers advanced slowly up the channel.

'It's getting deeper,' said the gruff voice.

The owner of it had passed the cave and stood exactly under Strongsoul, who thought he would be sure to hear his heart thumping against his ribs. He did not, however, and stepped from under Strongsoul.

'Hillo!' he cried, 'I'm up to the chin—and it grows deeper and deeper,' he added, having pushed his stick forward to test the bottom.

'What's to be done?'

'We must go back. One step more and I would be over the head.'

Here Strongsoul was unable to smother completely a laugh of exultation.

'What's that?' said one.

A kelpie, most likely,' said the gruff voice. ' The sooner we're out of here the better.'

Grumbling at such a wetting for nothing they all turned and left the passage. Strongsoul followed them along the ledge and into the open glen, when they had gone away a piece. He had no boots on, and therefore made no noise. He was not accustomed to go about with bare feet, so he had to be very careful not to hurt them on the stones.

The four men were met by four others at the cleft where the giant's cave was, and the eight sat down on the stones and began to talk in whispers. Strongsoul crept quietly up until he was able to hear what they were saying. He was overjoyed to learn from their talk that they were searching for the giant to take him and his into custody. So he spoke up boldly and said, ' Ye search for the giant Grislybeard.'

' The devil !' said the owner of the gruff voice.

' No ; I am the pilgrim Strongsoul bound for the City of Destruction. Who are ye ? '

' It's the kelpie,' said the gruff-voiced man in alarm, and the whole eight crowded together against the rock.

' What do ye fear ? ' said Strongsoul. ' Are ye not also pilgrims ? '

'Speak to it, somebody,' said the gruff-voiced man.

'We're no meanin' any harm tae ye, Maister Kelpie, or mebbe I should say Miss—I dinna ken what sex ye're o',' some one said. 'But we'll be muckle obleeged tae ye if ye'll tell us whaur this cave is. We've searched the hills hereaboots for weeks but we canna find it.'

'The cave is right above us,' said Strongsoul.

Nobody replied to this.

'It is,' said Strongsoul, understanding their silence to mean doubt. 'Inside this crack on the left about half way up is the entrance. It's very difficult to get at.'

'We'll have to risk a light,' said the gruff-voiced man.

One of the others took a small lantern from his pocket, and lighting it turned it on Strongsoul.

'I declare it's a laddie!' said two or three in a breath.

The gruff-voiced man who seemed to be the leader seized him by the collar.

'Hands off!' said Strongsoul.

The man looked at him closely and shook him a little; but Strongsoul, who had picked up a broken branch, struck him on the head with it, and the man let go his hold more amazed than hurt.

'I believe it is a kelpie,' he said. 'They can look like what they please.'

'If he can show us the cave,' said the man with the light, 'it doesn't matter what he is.'

'That's true,' said the leader. 'Where is it?'

Strongsoul pointed them the place as well as he could by the light of the lantern.

'How do they get up to it?' asked the leader.

Strongsoul explained about the windlass, and told them, seeing that they were friendly, of the capture by Grislybeard, and how Saunders had been carried off, and how he himself had escaped. They all wondered at the story, but nobody made any remark. They looked up the rock, straining their eyes, for the lantern gave a feeble light. Then they stared at Strongsoul and then at each other.

At length the leader said, 'We can't do any more to-night. We'll come with a ladder to-morrow and see how much of this is true.'

Strongsoul remembered stumbling over a fallen larch-tree on the road up with the giant. It struck him that they might use it as a ladder, and he made the proposal. The leader looked at him admiringly, and whispered to the man with the lantern, 'I'm sure it's a kelpie.'

Strongsoul led them down the glen, and they

were not long in coming to the fallen larch. Six of
them hoisted it on their shoulders and carried it up
to the cleft. They broke off all the longer branches,
leaving a bit of each to climb by, and then they
wedged the tree in the entrance, placing the top
against the left side and the trunk against the right,
so that it stood pretty steadily. To make it surer
three of them held it.

'Now,' said the leader, 'will you go up first?'

He looked to the place where he had last seen
Strongsoul, but he was not there.

'I told ye,' he said with some complacence.
'It's just a kelpie. It'll not be me that'll go up that
tree.'

'Nor me,' said one, and then another, and then
all of them, finding that nobody pretended to bravery
in the matter.

'Kelpies,' said one, 'are kittle cattle. I've heard
o' gey mishanters happenin' folk that lippen't tae
them. I had a gudebrither wha gaed oot ae nicht
an' forgaither't wi' ane at a well. He was a bauld
eneuch falla', for he merrit my sister, bein' my gude-
brither, ye see. An' my sister had a temper like a
nor'-east wun', an' hands like hammers, an' likit a
dram tae. She took after her mither, an' her faither
forbye. Geordie, ye min' my faither? Ay, an' d'ye

min' yon time you an' me frichten't my auntie? Man——'

'Well, here I am,' said Strongsoul, appearing suddenly, and cutting short the story of the gude-brither and the kelpie and the man's sister, etc. 'I've been putting on stockings and boots to climb the tree.'

No one said a word and Strongsoul began to mount. As he went up the leader noticed that his boots were dripping wet. He pointed it out to the man with the lantern and whispered, 'Ye may be sure it's a kelpie now. Who but a kelpie would keep his boots in the water!'

Strongsoul climbed about half-way up the tree and then told them that he couldn't get any further without more light.

'Well,' said the leader to the others, 'shall we risk it?'

'It's no use,' said the man with the lantern, 'attempting concealment now. If there were people up there they must have heard us long ago and be miles away by this time.'

'But if this is the only entrance?' said the leader.

'There's no likelihood of that,' replied the other. 'It's a poor mouse that has only one way to its hole.'

'Well, then, light the torches,' cried the leader, letting out the full volume of his gruff voice.

Six torches were soon ablaze, lighting up a space of the night, which thronged so thick and dark where

the radiance died that it crowded out all the stars. Strong-soul looked down and was glad to see the faces of the men. He looked up and was equally glad to see that the mouth of the cave was just above him. In a minute he stood in it, and bending over said, 'I'm up now, but the windlass is away.'

'Who goes next?' said the leader.

After some talking it was decided that the four men who had been in the water, and who were shivering with cold, should climb the tree for the sake of the exercise, and that the other four should

hold it at the bottom.   When the exploring party
were all up two of them who had extinguished their
torches and brought them in their pockets re-lit them.
Strongsoul led the way into the cave with a beating
heart.

The passage was about twenty feet long, and
sloped so much and so irregularly that they had to
walk warily.   They were all more or less tremulous,
but they heard nothing except the echoes of their
own steps.   When they came to the cave they stood
and peered into it.   The two torches were quite
sufficient to light up its walls and floor, but the roof
besides being high was concealed by a cloud of
smoke.   Seeing nobody—much to Strongsoul's
astonishment, who had expected to find the giant
and his men in order of battle—they ventured in
and looked about them.

'Here's the still, and a big one too,' said the
leader, laying his hand on a large copper kettle with
a long bent horn of the same metal rising out of it,
the like of which Strongsoul had never seen before.
'And I declare it's hot!' he cried excitedly.
Looking down, he saw a fire of peat smouldering
between the two stones on which the still sat.

Strongsoul with horror in his eyes examined this,
to him, strange utensil.   He saw that the horn was

joined to a pipe which twisted round about the inside
of a small barrel full of water, and that the water
was kept cool from a supply in another and larger
barrel standing on the top of a box.

'Oh me!' he cried, falling on his knees and bursting into tears, for he felt certain that Saunders had
been boiled in this huge kettle, and in some diabolical
manner pulled like a ribbon through the twisting
pipe.

'What ails ye?' said one of the men.

'Open it, please,' said Strongsoul, sobbing.

Two of the men unscrewed the horn from the
pipe and the kettle and lifted it off. Shaking in
every limb Strongsoul looked in, and was almost
knocked down by a strong smell. But it was not
the smell of boiled Saunders.

'What is this?' said Strongsoul.

'A still,' said the leader, 'for making whisky.'

Then Strongsoul perceived how Grislybeard
was steeped in iniquity. Not only did he waylay
and carry off pilgrims, but he was a maker and
diffuser of that deadly enemy of pilgrims—strong
drink.

Strongsoul's concern for Saunders was little
diminished by the knowledge that he had not been
despatched in the horrible way he had imagined.

He went over the whole cave, sounding the walls and the floors, and looking into some bags and barrels that lay about, but he could find no trace of his comrade. Nor could he see any way out of the cave except that by which they had entered. This forced him to the conclusion that Grislybeard and his men must have left the cave with Saunders and Mrs. Grislybeard some time before the arrival of the search-party.

In the meantime the men were discussing what they should do. They were not excise officers— merely ploughmen and railway porters belonging to the countryside who thought to make money by capturing an illicit still, a service for which Government pays a large sum.

'I think the gaugers break the still,' said the leader.

'Ay, but how are we to do it?' said another.

'I tell ye what,' put in a third. 'We can easily take away the worm and the horn. That'll be proof positive that we found a still here.'

'I believe that's the right way,' said the leader; 'it's not likely that the still 'll be removed before morning, and we can come back early and break it.'

'Suppose you pitch the still out of the cave,' said

Strongsoul. 'It would be smashed against the rocks.'

'The kelpie for ever!' cried the leader.

It took three of them to carry the still up the steep incline, while the fourth went before and told those below what was about to be done. The natural platform at the mouth of the cave extended a little way up the ravine, so that they were able to keep clear of the tree in pitching over the still. They threw it, clanging, against the opposite wall. It bounced back, and struck the side from which it was sent some yards down. Once again before reaching the bottom it crossed the space between the rocks, ringing out a hollow sound that echoed away up into the sky and seemed to fill the whole night. It fell with a dull crash right on the spot where the giantess had lain; and they knew that no more whisky would come from that still.

Having thrown the horn and the worm out into the glen, they descended one by one. When they were all down the leader cried, 'Three cheers for the kelpie!' But Strongsoul was nowhere to be seen. Nevertheless he insisted on the three cheers. How the shout rolled among the rocks and up and down the glen, cheering Strongsoul as he ran back to his cave!

One of the men twisted the worm round his body ; another blew a blast on the crooked horn ; and with torches ablaze, and in the best of spirits, the gallant eight went down the glen, laughing and singing, and speculating as to the amount of money to be divided among them.

CHAPTER V

IT was impossible for Strongsoul to sleep. He wanted to, because his brain was in a whirl, but just on that account sleep kept away from him. Where had Grislybeard taken Saunders, and what had he done with him? By what vent did the smoke of the fire get out of the cave? What had been done with the windlass and cage? In spite of himself these questions kept constantly in his mind. He lay for an hour with his eyes shut, but at the end of it sleep was as far away as ever. He sat up in despair, and opening his eyes perceived that day was dawning, for he was able to distinguish the entrance to his cave. It was very faintly marked—so faintly that, to make certain, he walked towards the oblong patch of darkness less dark than that which surrounded it, and nearly fell into the water; there could, therefore, be no doubt that it was the door. He stood in it, and was soon able to see the opposite rock, then the water, and, looking out, the entrance to the passage. Beyond in the open glen there was more light.

He ate some of his scones and cheese, and slinging his boots and stockings round his neck went into the glen. He had a pair of dry stockings, but his boots were so damp that he found it impossible to get them on. He placed his boots where he thought they would catch the sun, and then in his stocking-feet went to the giant's cleft. He crept down to the cracked still, and walked along as far as he could, but there was no appearance of any second opening into the cave. Hardly had he turned to go back when he heard voices, and then a crash. He was too far from the mouth of the cleft to see who were the speakers, but he noticed that the tree had fallen. Very glad he was now that he hadn't his boots on, for he was able to walk without making any noise. The path was littered with stones and rocks, which made it necessary for him to watch his steps. About half-way back to the mouth of the cleft he looked up. There, on the platform, stood Grislybeard and two men planting the windlass. Strongsoul crouched down behind a large rock and watched.

As soon as the windlass was adjusted Grislybeard and one of the men went back into the cave, and

returned shortly, carrying Mrs. Grislybeard. Strongsoul heard her groan, so he knew, much to his regret,
that he hadn't killed her. Grislybeard placed her in
the cage, and putting one foot on either side and
holding on by the chain bade the men lower away.
From where Strongsoul lay it was impossible to see
the cage reach the ground. Soon, however, the men
began to wind it up. Two others had appeared by
this time, each with a little barrel in his arms. These
two entered the cage the moment it reached the
platform and were rapidly lowered. When the cage
had been wound up again the men undid the windlass and took everything back to the cave. Strongsoul began to creep along the ravine with the
intention of following Grislybeard when he saw the
tree erected again, and in a little while the other men
reappeared and descended by it.

Where was Saunders? In the cave, alive or
dead—Strongsoul felt certain of that. It must be a
double cave, he thought, and they had failed to find
the way into the second one in their search during
the night. Why had Grislybeard left the tree
standing? To this question also he found an answer
which satisfied himself: to have left the tree on the
ground would have been a sign that the smugglers
had been at the cave since the search-party visited it.

Strongsoul took out his book and read the account
of the siege of Doubting Castle, and of the deaths of
Giant Despair and his wife Diffidence.   Then he
advanced boldly to the mouth of the cleft and climbed
the tree.   He walked straight into the cave and
searched it up and down.   Nothing was changed
since he saw it in the night, except that the smoke
was gone.   Looking up he saw a shaft of light
piercing the gloom near the roof.   It came through
the wall in which the entrance was, and the crevice
which admitted it he took to be the vent through
which the smoke escaped.   He sat down on a box
and considered.   An idea struck him like a flash.   He
followed with his eye the shaft of light, and saw that
it was not stopped by the side of the cave opposite
that through which it entered.   It was perfectly clear,
then, that the inner side did not reach the roof.   He
piled boxes and barrels on the top of each other, and
in that way got so far up.   Then, by means of holes
in the rock, not without some scratches, he succeeded
in reaching the top of the wall, which was about three
feet from the roof.   Finding that he could walk down
on the other side, he waited until his eyes were accustomed to the greater darkness.   He then began to
explore this second cave.

He found numerous barrels, a rope-ladder attached

to the wall and ready to fling over, the windlass and the cage, and, in a corner, Saunders. He knelt beside him and found that he was alive, but tied up with ropes and gagged. Strongsoul soon set him at liberty.

'It's me,' he said.

'Wha? You! Tak' me tae my granny.'

'Come, come,' said Strongsoul; 'I'll give you some whisky.'

Strongsoul knocked the bung into one of the barrels and made Saunders drink. The whisky revived him at once, and he began to collect his scattered senses.

'Man,' he said, 'I'm real glad tae see ye, but my banes are awfu' sair.'

He tried to stretch himself, but gave it up with a groan.

'We must get out of here,' said Strongsoul.

'Man, I'm real glad tae see ye,' said Saunders again. 'They tell't me that I would lie here till I dee't.'

'You'll tell me all about it when we get out,' said Strongsoul, flinging the rope-ladder over the wall. Saunders went down very shakily, Strongsoul keeping only two steps below him lest he should stumble. The next difficulty was the tree. Strongsoul went

down and held it at the bottom, and Saunders followed with many twinges and qualms, but he landed
all right, and was much the better of the exercise.
Difficulty number three was the getting into Strongsoul's cave.   At first Saunders flatly refused to
attempt it.   However, the sight of the ease and
agility with which Strongsoul moved along the ledge
gave him courage, and he found that it was as easy
as it seemed.   He was soon munching away at oat-
cake and cheese, while Strongsoul gave him a history
of his adventures since they parted.

Saunders had not so much to tell.   The giantess's
left leg and some of her ribs were broken.   They
had paid no attention to him until the still was set
agoing, and then the giant cross-questioned him,
slapping him in the face, and pinching his arms and
pulling his ears when he wouldn't answer.   Finally
they flung him in a corner with a crust of bread,
while they supped on cold meat and whisky.   They
talked low, but Saunders heard enough to understand
that they were discussing how to procure surgical
assistance for the giantess, and the prospects of their
illicit trade.   While they were still at supper he fell
into an uneasy sleep, from which he was awakened
by the giant pulling his arm violently.   They made
him ascend the ladder into the second cave, and

there they gagged him. He heard everything that was said and done by the search-party, and tried till his heart was like to burst to cry out to Strongsoul. It was after the search-party had left the cave that they tied him up and told him to lie there and die. He heard confusedly the noise of the departure of the smugglers, but remembered nothing with distinctness from the time they bound him until Strongsoul untied him. His story ended, Saunders said, 'An' noo I think we should ging hame.'

Strongsoul stared at him in blank amazement. Were they not having adventures of a much more extraordinary kind than they had dared to hope for —at least until they came to the City of Destruction? And had not he, Saunders, already earned a high rank among pilgrims by his cruel sufferings? Saunders had forgotten that point of view and was staggered a little.

'But what's it a' tae end in?' he asked.

'End in!' cried Strongsoul; 'the Celestial City. But before that the Land of Beulah. We shall get there while we are still boys, and there we shall fall in love with beautiful girls and marry them, and, like Christiana's children, live there for a long time before crossing the river. Listen,' cried Strongsoul, and he opened his book and read.

Here Cosmo took from his pocket a little dumpy book, and holding it out said, 'This was the book that Strongsoul took on his pilgrimage.' Then, having found the place, he said, 'This is the passage he read to Saunders.' And he read as follows :—

'" After this I beheld until they were come into the Land of Beulah, where the sun shineth night and day. Here because they were weary they took themselves a while to rest. And because the country was common to pilgrims, and because the orchards and vineyards that were here belonged to the king of the Celestial country, therefore they were licensed to make bold with any of his things. But a little while soon refreshed them here : for the bells did so ring and the trumpets continually sound so melodiously that they could not sleep, and yet they received as much refreshing as if they had slept their sleep ever so soundly. Here also the noise of them that walked the streets was, More pilgrims have come to town ! And another would answer, saying, And so many went over the water and were let in at the golden gates to-day ! They would cry again, There is now a legion of shining ones just come to town, by which we know that there are more pilgrims upon the road ; for here they come to wait for them, and to comfort them after their sorrow ! Then the pilgrims got up and walked to and fro. But how were their ears now filled with heavenly voices, and their eyes delighted with celestial visions! In this land they heard nothing, saw nothing, felt nothing, smelt nothing, tasted nothing, that was offensive to their stomach or mind; only when they tasted of the water of the river over which they were to go they thought that it tasted a little bitterish to the palate, but it proved sweet when it was down.

' " In this place the children of the town would go into the king's gardens, and gather nosegays for the pilgrims, and bring them to them with much affection. Here also grew camphire with spikenard and saffron, calamus and cinnamon, with all the trees of frankincense, myrrh and aloes with all chief spices. With these the pilgrims' chambers were perfumed while they stayed here; and with these were their bodies anointed to prepare them to go over the river when the time appointed was come." '

Strongsoul's voice thrilled through Saunders in this reading. His face shone, and his eyes burned so brightly that Saunders was ashamed to look at him.

'Will you come?' he said.

I will,' replied Saunders.

Then they both lay down and slept, and dreamt of the Land of Beulah, and of beautiful little girls with golden hair and earnest blue eyes who brought them bunches of grapes and peaches, and sweet-smelling flowers; and when they awoke it was almost noon.   They bathed themselves in the stream, ate the remainder of the provisions the goodwife had given them, and set out on their travels once more.   They left the glen as soon as possible and climbed to the shoulder of the hill. Looking south-east in the direction of the City of Destruction they spied in the distance a large and fair building, which reminded Strongsoul of the Palace Beautiful.

'It is certainly a palace,' he said.   'We will journey towards it.'

Straight across hill and dale they took their way, and as they went they talked.

'Saunders,' said Strongsoul, 'have you been thinking lately of Weights and Measures?'

'I gie ye my word,' said Saunders, 'they havena' crossed my mind sin' we met the giant.   Twa mair days like yesterday an' I wouldna' ken the differ atween *Troy Weight* an' *Square Measure.*'

'We shall have many days like yesterday,' said Strongsoul; but seeing Saunders's face fall he added,

'I mean as full of adventures—not that you'll ever suffer so much again.'

'Man, I canna' see what's the gude o' this sufferin'.'

'It's to make us strong and hardy, and enjoy the land of Beulah and the Celestial City all the more when we come to them.   All the good that's in people is brought out by their having to suffer— anyway it ought to be.'

'Eh, man!' cried Saunders.   'I've heard my granny say somethin' like that, but she'd little hope o' me.   She used tae say I mindit her o' a proverb, "Mash snaw an' mask it, ye'll hae but water."   She was aye hard on me, my granny.'

'I never had a granny,' said Strongsoul.

'Weel, ye needna' compleen.   My granny has a rhyme that she's aye comin' owre—

> '"Gin ye're an anvil, haud ye still ;
>   Gin ye're a hammer, smite yer fill."

And she's been a hammer sin' I kenned her, an' a'body else is anvils.'

Strongsoul laughed at this, and told Saunders that he ought to be glad, because many pilgrims had to forsake people whom they liked a great deal better than he did his granny.

'Oh, but she's no a bad body, mind ye,' said Saunders. 'She kens a thing or twa, an' she's crouse eneuch tae, if she wouldna' be juist sae camstairie.'

'By the bye,' said Strongsoul, 'have you had any dreams?'

'Aboot a new name?'

'Yes.'

'Na; it's no likely, noo, that my name will be changed till we come to the City o' Destruction,' said Saunders. 'But dae ye think there's muckle truth in dreams?'

'All the dreams of pilgrims come true,' said Strongsoul.

'Dae they, man?'

'Oh yes!'

They were silent for a little. Then Saunders said, 'An' thae wee lassies in the Land o' Beuley.'

'What about them?'

'Man,' said Saunders with some hesitation, coming close up to Strongsoul, 'I dreamt aboot them.'

Now Strongsoul had dreamt about them too, but he only said, 'And what did you dream?'

'Oh, no muckle; juist what you read. A lassie wi' gowden hair an' blue een cam' tae me cannily, an' gied me a flo'or an' a bunch o' grapes, an'

smiled couthily, an' syne gaed awa' lookin' owre
her shouther.   An', man, she was bonny, an' I
likit her, an' I never could be fashed wi' lassies

afore.   What dae ye think is the meanin' o' my
dream ? '

'I think it means that you will some day like
girls.'

'Dae ye ? '

'Yes.'

'Man, I'll be glad o' that ; for they're bonny bit things—thae in the Land o' Beuley.'

Then Strongsoul told his dream, which was pretty much like Saunders's ; and they walked along arm-in-arm saying nothing, but with flushed faces thinking about the little blue-eyed girls in the Land of Beulah.

Hunger put an end to their day-dream. The palace was still a long way off, and Strongsoul's feet were tired and sore, for his boots had been dried in the sun till they were as hard as horn. He sank down, saying, 'I must have a rest.'

'An' I maun hae somethin' tae eat,' cried Saunders.

He climbed up a little higher than they were, but there was no house in sight except the palace. He saw that the way to it would be much shortened if they were to return to the road. So he hailed Strongsoul, who clambered up beside him, and agreed with him that they ought to get back to the highway. They both took off their boots and stockings, and found it very pleasant scampering down the hillside, the very idea of the change from the hill to the once-despised highway giving them new strength. Strongsoul felt particularly delighted at his own delight in getting back to the narrow way.

They found it much more agreeable than it had

been the day before, because there were trees on both sides—fine old chestnuts whose branches met and made a roof as far as they could see. The sun came through in showers and spots and splatches. There was no wind, and the dust lay on the road like a thick Brussels carpet. They amused themselves by walking now in the sunshine, now in the shadow, the difference in the heat of the dust being always wonderful to them. A mile of this road, which did not tire them in the least, brought them to the porter's lodge. They washed their feet in a stream by the wayside and put on their boots, and tried to make themselves look as decent as possible. But Strongsoul's clothes were torn, and poor Saunders's, besides being torn, were very threadbare. Then their faces were black and blue, and yellow and green, with the blows they had given each other in their first encounter, and the knocks they had received in their fight with Grislybeard. It was no wonder that the woman who came out of the porter's lodge as they entered the gate looked at them suspiciously. Strongsoul approached her quite unconscious of anything odd in his conduct or appearance—for pilgrims must become travel-stained and wayworn—and asked what was the name of the palace.

' What'n a palace ? ' said the woman.

' Are you not the portress ? ' asked Strongsoul.

The woman looked at them stupidly. Strongsoul then asked her if the porter was in. Again the woman made no reply, and Strongsoul being at the end of his questions turned from her and started up the avenue with Saunders. The woman gazed at them for a minute, and then ran after them, and seized Strongsoul by the collar and said, ' Ye canna' go up.'

' How ? We are pilgrims,' said Strongsoul.

' It doesna' matter. Ye canna' go up.'

The woman looked very determined, but Strongsoul gave her the sixpence which the goodwife had given him. Amazed at receiving money from one whom she supposed a beggar she let them go.

The avenue was long and uphill, and they were out of breath when they arrived at the courtyard. On entering it they found a great bustle : so busy was everybody that they were unnoticed for a time.

The palace was in two divisions, one old and one new ; and there was a very magnificent terraced garden in front of it, which Strongsoul and Saunders couldn't enough admire. In it there was being erected a great white tent. Arches were going up in the courtyard and in the gateway, and garlands

of flowers were being hung over doors and in
windows.   They saw a man going about very
authoritatively, and they thought of addressing him,
when a tall and dignified gentleman entered the
courtyard from the modern building and talked to
the authoritative individual, who listened with great
humility.   The dignified gentleman having given his
instructions was about to retire when Strongsoul
with Saunders at his heels stepped in his way.

'Sir,' said Strongsoul, 'are you the keeper of this
palace?'

The dignified gentleman looked at the pilgrims
impassively, and turned round as if to summon the
authoritative individual, but he thought better of it
and said coldly, 'I am, if you call it a palace.'

'Is it not a palace then?' asked Strongsoul.

The dignified gentleman again turned towards
the authoritative individual, who was watching the
interview some yards off, evidently anticipating a
summons to remove Strongsoul and Saunders; but
again the gentleman changed his mind.   Something
in Strongsoul's face—something of earnestness,
bordering on passion, for we know what a devoted
pilgrim Strongsoul was—attracted him, so he said
less coldly, 'This is Moredun Castle.'

'And are pilgrims entertained here?'

'What do you mean?'

'This is the pilgrim Saunders Elshander, and I am the pilgrim Strongsoul. We are on our way to the City of Destruction; and, sir, we have had nothing to eat except some bread and cheese since last night. We thought that this was a place for the refreshment of pilgrims, so we came here.'

During this little speech Saunders was doing his best to hide behind Strongsoul, but being fully a foot taller had no very great success. He watched the expression of the keeper's face, and was in the act of twitching Strongsoul's sleeve and running off when the keeper said, 'How long have you been pilgrims?'

'Since yesterday morning, sir.'

'And where do you come from?'

'From Dunmyatt.'

'But that's not so very far away. You can't have been all this time coming from Dunmyatt.'

'No, sir. We were taken captive by Giant Grislybeard, and Saunders was kept a prisoner all night.'

'Who is Giant Grislybeard? But come in.'

The keeper of the palace or castle preceded them, and led them through a great hall into a room full of books and pictures.

'You are hungry, I think,' he said.

'Yes, sir,' said Strongsoul.

'You will have something to eat immediately.'

He was about to leave the room when a little girl entered. She stood stock-still with amazement on seeing the pilgrims, and they returned her gaze with intense interest. The little lady was not quite so tall as Strongsoul ; she had beautiful golden hair and blue eyes, and in a basket which she carried were some lovely flowers.

'These are two pilgrims, Pansy,' said the keeper of the castle. 'They are on their way to the City of Destruction, and they are hungry, and we must give them something to eat.'

'Oh, papa !' cried Pansy. 'Pilgrims ! Just like *The Pilgrim's Progress ?*'

'It seems so,' said the keeper, with a smile.

'But it can't be,' said Pansy. 'Are you real and true pilgrims ?' she said to Strongsoul.

'Yes ; we are pilgrims on our way through the City of Destruction to the Land of Beulah and the Celestial City,' said Strongsoul eagerly, and Pansy was convinced.

'How delightful !' she said. 'Oh, papa, let me look after them.'

'Very well. I hope you will excuse me,' said the

keeper, turning to the pilgrims ; 'I am very busy. My daughter will see that you are attended to.'

When the keeper had left the room Pansy said, 'Now, what would you like to eat?'

'Just what you are in the habit of giving pilgrims,' said Strongsoul.

'But we have never had pilgrims before,' said Pansy. 'What would you like?' addressing Saunders.

'Weel, mem,' said Saunders with considerable diffidence, 'a cog o' parritch an' a bit ham an' egg would dae me.'

This was the height of luxury in eating hitherto attained by Saunders, and that on two occasions when he had breakfasted with his master, the grocer. He referred to it now because he wished to let the little lady know that he had some acquaintance with good living. Pansy lifted and laid one foot after the other like a little restive pony, and winked and flashed her eyes at the broad Scotch.

'I think I'll have to give you what there is to get. That'll be the best way,' she said.

'Verra weel, mem,' said Saunders. 'We're no ill tae please.'

'Do you always speak like that?' asked Pansy, for in her ears Saunders's speech was coarse and vulgar.

Q

Saunders blushed and looked sheepish, and Pansy was sorry. She was about to speak when she noticed her flowers, and lifting a lily in her rosy hand she gave it to Saunders, looking a sweet apology. Saunders couldn't speak, but he made a very low

bow, unlike anything Pansy had ever seen, but not at all awkward, quite simple and expressive. She gave Strongsoul a red rose, beside which her rosy hand looked a lily ; and Strongsoul did as Saunders had done, feeling that it was more beautiful to do so than to speak.

As Pansy left the room she looked over her shoulder and smiled. The moment she had gone Saunders and Strongsoul, sighing together a great long-pent sigh, turned and saw in one another's eyes that each had beheld his dream.

Pansy was some time in returning, because she found it difficult to get anybody to attend to her

orders, so busy were they with their festive pre-
parations ; and then when she had secured the
services of a boy who knew more about the stable
than the dining-room, her nurse laid hold of her and
dressed her for riding. She rebelled at first, but
nurse told her, knowing how much she loved her
father, that he had been very particular in arranging
that she should have her ride in spite of the turmoil
in which the castle was : Pansy was a delicate girl,
and was also the Lady Violet Moredun, daughter of
the Duke of Moredun—his only child—and the
doctor had ordered her to ride every day for her
health. Her mother had been dead for several years,
and the relations between father and daughter were
most intimate and affectionate.

When Pansy got back to the pilgrims she burst
out laughing. The table was spread, and the pilgrims
sat at it, but neither of them had dared to touch anything. The boy who waited on them stood behind
Saunders's chair with a cover in his hand and a nap-
kin in his mouth to cork back the laughter. Pansy's
laughter made him laugh out too—the pilgrims
looked so ridiculous sitting there as stiff as pokers
with their hands on their knees and faces of great
solemnity, blushing at the beautiful plates and the
silver knives and forks.

'You may go,' Pansy said to the servant, and he left the room.

'Eat, eat,' she said. 'I'm sure you're hungry. Eat a great lot—eat everything. Nobody will come here until I return from my ride.' She swept out of the room in her riding-habit like the little lady she was.

Saunders and Strongsoul tried to follow the instructions of Pansy, but failed to do anything more than diminish slightly the good things provided for them. Having eaten as much as they could, and more than was good for them, they looked out of the window and watched the bustle in the garden. An hour passed, and they were beginning to be restless when they noticed a commotion. All the servants and workmen rushed up the terrace, evidently making for the courtyard. The pilgrims, fearing that something had happened to Pansy, ran out of the castle to learn what was the matter.

The groom who had ridden with Pansy stood frightened and breathless in the centre of a crowd telling the duke something. The pilgrims pushed forward within hearing, and the duke said as the groom finished his story, 'I don't understand you.'

He was very white, and he would have fallen had not a gentleman who stood beside him caught him in his arms. The gentleman was Lord Francis Lear-mont, the duke's brother.

'What is it?' said the duke to the groom. 'Tell me again.'

Then the groom told how the Lady Violet had ridden along a favourite road of hers which led out of the policies into a great wood ; how, shortly after they had entered the wood, his horse shrieked and fell, and he himself was clutched by two men and his eyes bandaged, but not before he had seen the Lady Violet's horse fall also and two other men lay hold of her ; how he had been held there for some time and then dragged away into the wood and left lying in a thicket with his hands tied ; how he managed to slip his hands out of the rope, and after some searching had found his way back to the road where both horses lay hamstrung ; and how he had then run straight to the castle without a halt.

'It can't be,' said the duke. 'It's impossible. Such things aren't done nowadays.'

The groom called God to witness that it was true : the horses were there in the road to prove it.

Strongsoul waited to hear no more. He pulled Saunders by the sleeve and they moved out of the crowd.

'Get the pillowslip,' said Strongsoul.

Saunders ran into the house and brought it.

The lowest room in the old tower was an armoury, and the door of it stood open. Strongsoul went in and took two naked swords. These he wrapped in the pillowslip, and followed by the wondering Saunders set off running to the highway. At first they ran so quickly that Saunders for lack of breath could put no question, but when they had to slacken their pace he inquired where they were going.

'To the cave,' said Strongsoul. 'This is Grisly-beard's work.'

'Hoo dae ye ken?' said Saunders.

'I don't know how I know, but I know.'

Saunders felt that there was nothing more to be said, so he took the pillowslip from Strongsoul to give him a rest, and they marched along together with white resolute faces. As soon as they were out of the highway Strongsoul took the pillowslip and threw it away, and they went up the glen sword in hand. To Saunders's surprise they had not the least difficulty in finding the road ; but Strongsoul was not at all astonished, for he knew that the steps of pilgrims, when they are on an enterprise such as they had undertaken, are specially directed.

Strongsoul made Saunders keep at some distance behind him as they drew near the cave, so that if

one were taken the other might escape; but they
arrived at the cleft without meeting any one. The
tree was down, and on going up the glen a little way
they saw that the windlass had been placed on the
platform. By this they knew that Grislybeard and
his men were in the cave—with Pansy, Strongsoul
was certain.

'What'll we dae noo?' asked Saunders.

'Go down the glen and hide behind a tree. If
Grislybeard hasn't found out your escape by this
time he will soon, and then he will know that the
inner cave has been discovered.'

'An' what then?'

'Then they'll leave the cave. Don't you see?'

'An' what'll we dae?'

'Attack them as they pass.'

'A' richt,' said Saunders, flourishing his sword.

Just then sounds came from the platform, so they
hurried down the glen and got in behind some alder
bushes. In a few minutes they heard the footsteps
of a man approaching.

'You jump out behind him. I'll jump in front of
him,' said Strongsoul. 'Stop! One—two—three!'
and the man was between the points of their
swords.

'Stand!' cried Strongsoul; but there was no

need, for the man stood still enough in the utmost amazement.

'Have they discovered the escape of Saunders?'

No answer.

'Have they discovered the escape of Saunders?'

Still no answer.

'Speak, or I'll run you through.'

At this moment Saunders in his excitement pricked the man in the back. He writhed and was in the act of crying out, but Strongsoul touched him on the breast, saying, 'And if you shout I'll run you through.'

'What do you want?' said the man angrily.

'Speak quietly, or I'll run you through,' said Strongsoul.

Again Saunders unintentionally pricked him, and the man wheeled about.

'What do you mean?' he cried.

'I'll rin ye through,' said Saunders.

Then Strongsoul in his turn pricked him in the back, and he span round with a curse.

'You're to talk to me,' said Strongsoul. 'Have they discovered the escape of Saunders?'

'Yes.'

'Where are you going?'

'To my house.'

'What for?'

'My supper.'

'That's not true.'

Saunders raised his eyebrows; Strongsoul nodded, and the man got another prick in the back. If it had been planned and rehearsed it couldn't have been more prompt.

'Every time you tell a lie you'll be jagged in the back,' said Strongsoul. 'What are you going home for?'

'For a pick and a spade,' said the man surlily.

'What are you going to do with them?'

'I'm going to dig.'

'Dig what?'

'Potatoes.'

'With a pick!' said Strongsoul, nodding to Saunders, who at once stuck the point of his sword into the man for the fourth time. He was in the act of turning round when Strongsoul pricked him in the right arm.

'Every time you turn round I'll jag you,' said Strongsoul.

The man sank down on the ground swearing terribly. Had he been courageous, at the expense of a cut or two he could have overcome both boys; but he recognised Saunders, and he guessed who

Strongsoul was, and feared him, knowing how he had attacked Grislybeard and foiled the giantess.

'What are you going to do with the pick and spade?' asked Strongsoul.

'Dig a grave.'

'Whose grave?'

The man was silent for a second or two; then he said, 'Jenny's.'

'Who's Jenny?'

'The boss's wife.'

'Oh, Mrs. Grislybeard!'

Strongsoul nodded, and Saunders quickly performed his part. The man sprang to his feet, but in doing so he received the points of both swords and sank to the ground again.

'Whose grave?'

'The Lady Violet Moredun's.'

'Is she dead?'

'No; she's to be killed when I come back.'

'Why is she to be killed? Come, tell the whole story or we'll kill you.'

'Lord Francis Learmont,' said the man, squeezing the words out, 'will be the duke's sole heir when the Lady Violet's out of the way. He's given five hundred pounds to us to do the job. Her throat's to be cut and she's to be buried up there, and we're all to **cut to** America—that **is, us** four. There's **other** two that **don't** know anything about **it, and if** the body's found they'll get the blame. It's the safest thing ever done if it **weren't for you.'** The man cursed them again and again.

'**How** many **men** are there in the cave **just** now ?'

' Three.'

'**That makes four** with **you ; but** there were five **last night.'**

'**Ay,** but **he's not in** the secret. **We had to** set **the** still agoing last night **on** his account, curse him. **Even with** that **he** suspected something.'

'Get up and take off your coat and **hat.'**

The man did so, and Strongsoul slipped them on **without** putting **his arms** into **the sleeves of** the coat. Having ordered Saunders to his side he said to the man, 'If you speak or move without my orders we'll both plunge **our** swords into you. Forward.'

A yard from the cleft Strongsoul halted them. He went into the entrance and made the man stand behind him with **the** point **of** Saunders's sword touching the back of his neck.

'You're to whistle,' said Strongsoul, 'and when **they answer** cry out, " Take me up at once ; there are people in the glen." But if you let the tip of your nose be seen Saunders will run you through.'

The prisoner whistled thrice and the answer came. When the men appeared above Strongsoul looked up, having the hat pulled down over his brows and shading his face with his hand. The prisoner shouted as he had been instructed, and the cage came down at once. Strongsoul jumped in and they drew him up. The moment he reached the platform he threw off the coat and hat, and springing out of the cage stabbed one of the men in the side. He fell shrieking. The other turned and ran, but Strongsoul followed him, and making up on him drove his sword through his right thigh so that he also fell with a prolonged shriek, for Strongsoul had some difficulty in withdrawing the blade. When his sword was free he ran forward and met Grisly-beard at the entrance of the cave. The giant was armed with a heavy iron bar.

'You? Ha, ha! I've got ye now!' he cried, heaving up his weapon.

Strongsoul rushed in under the blow and received the bar on his left shoulder, but so near the giant's hand that he hardly felt it; at the same time he cut the giant's left leg and got past him into the cave. He looked about, but he could not see the duke's daughter.   She had crept behind the water-barrel.

'Pansy!' he cried.

She looked out, and recognising Strongsoul ran towards him.

'Oh, dear pilgrim,' she said, 'take me home!'

'I will,' said Strongsoul.   'Stand back and watch the fight.'

She ran to a corner and falling on her knees clasped her hands and prayed.

Grislybeard bore down on Strongsoul, swinging the bar with great rapidity from side to side. Strongsoul could see no way of getting at him and retreated slowly.   The giant's intention was to force him against a wall, and press the breath out of him. This Strongsoul perceived, and keeping his eyes fixed on the giant's sprang up into the air about half his own height.   This action had just the effect he intended.   The giant, surprised for a second, ceased swinging his bar, and Strongsoul darting in wounded him so severely in the right hand that he let his weapon drop.   It was now the giant's turn to retreat.   He ran in behind the water-barrel and Strongsoul after him.   They went round the barrel and the fireplace several times until the giant who was fleeter than Strongsoul had put such a distance between them that he had time to stoop and pick up one of the stones of the fireplace. With this he ran to one side of the cave and stood at bay.

'Come on!' he cried, holding the stone above his head with both hands.

Strongsoul moved towards him warily, but without flinching. The blood was streaming from the wound in the giant's hand, and he felt his strength giving way. He determined, therefore, to strike while he had still the power to direct his huge missile. Strongsoul paused in his advance, measuring the distance between the giant and himself. His plan was to run at Grislybeard as soon as he discharged the stone, avoiding it as he had avoided the stroke of the bar. Suddenly the giant with a shout took two steps forward and hurled the piece of rock with all his force ; and Strongsoul fell. But the giant's aim had been unsteady. The stone barely grazed the back of Strongsoul's head, and although his shoulders caught it a little more heavily he was unhurt. The giant stumbled down on him before he could rise and seized his throat—not with any great force, for he thought Strongsoul had received the full weight of the stone and would give him little more trouble. He grinned hideously as he said, 'You'll catch it now, my man, if there's any

life in you.'   Just as he said that Strongsoul passed
his sword through the giant's body, and with a long-
drawn howl, ending in a groan, Grislybeard rolled
over dead.   Then Strongsoul rose, and seizing him

by the hair of the head raised his sword to strike;
but Pansy running from her corner caught his arm.

'What are you going to do?' she said.

'Cut off his head.'

'Oh, don't do that!'

'Why not? Greatheart always did it when he killed a giant, and an angel told me in a dream that I was to be equal to Greatheart. There are two more in the passage,' said Strongsoul, his eyes blazing with triumph. 'I'll cut off their heads too.'

'But they're not dead,' said Pansy, pointing to the door of the cave.

Strongsoul looked, and saw where the two wounded men stood bleeding against the wall with ghastly faces.

'Then I must kill them,' he said.

'For God's sake don't!' both men cried feebly.

'Oh, pilgrim, you must be merciful!' said Pansy.

'Well,' said Strongsoul magnanimously, not altogether liking the idea of an attack on two wounded and defenceless men, 'I'll not kill them ; but I mean to cut off the giant's head,' and he twisted Grisly-beard's hair round his wrist.

'I'll never speak to you if you do,' said Pansy.

Strongsoul gazed at Pansy, and Pansy gazed at him. Slowly he let go the giant's hair, and wiped the blood from his sword on the giant's clothes.

'Take me home,' said Pansy, turning away.

R

With a sigh and a lingering look at the giant's head Strongsoul took Pansy's hand and led her to the entrance.

'Go in,' he said to the wounded men.

Supporting each other they limped with many groans to the box on which the water-barrel stood, and leaning against it sat down on the ground. They then tried to attend to each other's wounds.

'They are suffering,' said Strongsoul compassionately. 'Would it not be better to kill them and put them out of their pain?'

'No,' said Pansy. 'Let us be quick and send them a doctor.'

With some reluctance Strongsoul assented to this. He remembered how the giant had taken down Mrs. Grislybeard, but he was at a loss how to regulate the speed of the descent. Not for long, however. He found a rope in a corner, and made a loop on each end of it. These he put over the handles of the windlass, and holding the rope tightly was able to control in a measure the revolution of the cylinder. The last few feet they came down with a run, for the rope gave out, but neither were hurt.

'Hoo mony hae ye kill't?' were the first words Saunders said.

'Only one.'

'That'll be twa then, for I think I've kill't this one. He thocht he could win owre me, an' I had tae run him through.'

But the man said he was not dead.

'We'll send you a doctor, then,' said Strongsoul.

'I hope yer leddyship's nane the waur,' said Saunders to Pansy.

'I'm afraid I am,' she said. 'Will we be long in getting home?'

'Not long,' said Strongsoul cheerfully. 'Come, we'll help you.'

With some diffidence Pansy slipped her arms into the pilgrims'. The rough road soon made her hold tight and lean hard, and by the time they got to the highway she was laughing and chattering as if they had been returning from a holiday.

Whom should they meet almost as soon as they got to the road but some of the search-party of the night before, including the gruff-voiced leader!

'Here she is!' he cried.

Besides the search-party there were other people in the road, and a crowd was immediately formed round Pansy and the pilgrims.

'Stand aside!' said Strongsoul, raising his sword,

but Pansy touched his arm and told him that these were friends.

'That we are,' said the gruff-voiced man; 'all of us. Everybody round about's searching for you, my lady.'

'It's very kind of them,' said Pansy. 'How can we get to Moredun Castle?'

'I've a spring-cart,' said the man eagerly, 'if your ladyship 'll condescend to use it.'

'Oh, thank you!' cried Pansy. 'I'll only be too glad.'

'It's this way,' said the man, pointing to a stile.

Pansy and the pilgrims crossed the road.

'Are these little rascals coming too?' said the man.

Before Pansy could answer Strongsoul struck him over the shoulders with the flat of his sword.

'Don't call people rascals without knowing them,' he said.

'I declare,' said the man, rubbing his shoulder, 'it's the kelpie! And is this another?' he asked, pointing to Saunders.

'These are the young gentlemen that saved my life,' said Pansy. 'They are pilgrims, and they are going back with me to Moredun. There are three wounded men at the cave in the glen,' she added, addressing some of those who stood about. 'You must get a doctor and go to them——and a policeman too, I think.'

Headed by three of the members of the old search-party a crowd set off up the glen in obedience

to Pansy, while one or two went to the village of Moredun for the doctor.

The gruff-voiced man's house not being very far off he soon had his cart yoked and they got into it without delay. They took a back road and saw no one until they arrived at the castle.

Strongsoul helped Pansy down, and she took

his arm and Saunders's and walked into the hall.
There was only one footman to be seen, because all
the other servants were either engaged searching for
Pansy or in the kitchen or in attendance in other
rooms. The footman gazed in amazement, especially
at the swaggering gait of the gruff-voiced man, who
had followed the others into the castle. Pansy heard
him behind her and, turning, said, 'I thank you very
much. Papa will see you afterwards. Jones, will
you take him to the servants' room?'

The gruff-voiced man, rather crestfallen, had to
go away with the footman, while Pansy led Strongsoul and Saunders to the drawing-room. When they
entered it the pilgrims drew in their breath and
turned giddy with astonishment. It was a long,
broad, high-ceiled room, and the splendour of it such
as neither of them had ever imagined. A number
of ladies and gentlemen stood in it, and one lady
dressed in black sat near a window. To her the
duke, who could hardly stand, he was so shaken
with grief, had just finished telling of the abduction
of his daughter when Pansy and the pilgrims
entered.

'My lord duke,' said the lady, rising, 'you are a
brave man. You have stayed to welcome me when
your heart was wrung with this great anguish. I

shall never forget it, and I thank you from my heart. Go now : I shall not expect to see you again until you have found my sweet little Pansy.'

As the lady said this she saw Pansy and the pilgrims at the end of the room. She took a step forward and touching the shoulder of the duke, whose eyes were bent on the ground as he bowed profoundly, pointed to the three children. The duke turned and, forgetting in whose presence he was, ran to Pansy and clasped her in his arms with a great sobbing cry. He kissed her over and over and led her to the lady.

Pansy kissed the lady's hand and the lady kissed her on the cheek. Then Pansy, moving backwards, took the pilgrims by the hands and led them to the lady.

'This is the pilgrim Strongsoul,' said Pansy.

Strongsoul knelt down, and the lady gave him her hand.

'This is the pilgrim Saunders Elshander,' said Pansy.

Saunders knelt beside Strongsoul, and the lady gave him her hand also.

'Rise, good pilgrims,' said the lady, very much amused and interested.

Strongsoul and Saunders rose, and picking up

their swords, which they had laid on the floor when
they knelt, stood on either side of Pansy. All the
ladies and gentlemen gathered round excited and
curious.

The lady looked at the duke, and the duke looked
at Pansy, and Pansy said, 'If you please, your
majesty, it is a long story. May I tell it?'

And the lady said 'Yes.'

Then Pansy told everything that had happened
to herself, and everything that Saunders and Strongsoul had done for her; and when she came to the
death of Grislybeard everybody started.

The lady said to Strongsoul, 'Do you think it
was right to kill this man?'

'Yes,' said Strongsoul.

'Why?'

'Because if I hadn't killed him he would have
killed me, and because he was bad.'

'Would you kill everybody who is bad?'

'No,' said Strongsoul. 'Only those who will not
let others be good, and who are the enemies of
pilgrims.'

'But what if you have committed murder?' said
the lady.

'Murder?' said Strongsoul dubiously. 'If Greatheart was a murderer, so am I.'

'I acquit you,' said the lady, smiling.

Then Pansy finished her story, and the lady looked at both pilgrims with great admiration.

'Give me your sword,' she said to Strongsoul. 'You are a brave and noble boy,' said the lady

when she had the sword. 'I wish you to be a brave and noble man. What is your name?'

'Strongsoul.'

'And what is your first name?'

'That is all my name.'

'Surely not.'

Strongsoul told the lady the dream he had dreamt on the side of Dunmyatt, and the lady was charmed with him.

She talked in whispers for a minute or two with the duke, then she handed back the sword to Strongsoul, and taking a ring from her finger put it on his hand, saying, 'Since you have no first name you shall be my Lord Strongsoul of Dunmyatt, and when you are a man you may perhaps sit in the House of Lords and help to govern my people.'

Strongsoul bent low, and Pansy with her eyes dancing came and kissed him.

'And what is your name?' said the lady to Saunders.

'Saunders Elshander, mem.

'Give me your sword, Saunders, and kneel down.'

Then the lady struck him on the shoulders with his sword and said, 'Rise, Sir Saunders Elshander'; and Sir Saunders jumped up, and the lady gave him his sword again. Pansy did not kiss Saunders, but she pressed his hand very warmly.

'And now, my lord,' said the lady to the duke, 'do you know who has done or instigated this thing?'

The duke did not know; but Lord Strongsoul

told the lady what he had heard about Lord Francis Learmont.

'Where is Lord Francis?' said the lady.

'He is leading the search,' said the duke, who seemed even more distressed at the news of his brother than he had been at the abduction of Pansy.

'Let Lord Francis Learmont come to me as soon as he returns,' said the lady.

Then they all went to dinner. The lady made Lord Strongsoul of Dunmyatt and Sir Saunders Elshander sit on her right hand and on her left, and she talked to them during the dinner about their pilgrimage. Now the lady knew *The Pilgrim's Progress* quite well, and so she said to them, 'My Lord Strongsoul of Dunmyatt and Sir Saunders Elshander, as you know, I am the queen of these countries, and I also am a pilgrim. I have, therefore, a great interest in the welfare of all pilgrims, and I wish very much that your pilgrimage should be successful. If you remember in *The Pilgrim's Progress* there are no boys who travel alone; they are either in the company of their parents, or of a guardian like Greatheart. Now there are erected in most of the towns in my dominions Interpreters' Houses, called schools and colleges, where young people, whether they have parents or not, are pre-

pared for pilgrimage, and I have been thinking that,
if you are willing, it would be wise of you to have
the instructions of one of these Interpreters before
going farther.'

Strongsoul bowed, and Saunders who took the
cue from him did likewise. Saunders expected
Strongsoul to say something, but as his leader kept
silence he ventured a remark of his own.

'Mem,' he said, 'my faither's a shepherd, an'
forbye that, as my granny says, ye micht as weel try
tae shave an egg as get a bawbee oot o' him if he
can keep it at all.'

The lady smiled graciously on Saunders, and he
was about to follow up what he deemed a brilliant
beginning with some more family matters and quota-
tions from his granny—for he was anxious to go to
college, and wished to explain that he would require
help—when the lady engaged the duke in conversation, and Saunders did not find another opportunity
of stating his mind.

'Saunders,' whispered Strongsoul as they passed
along a corridor after dinner, 'follow me.'

With some difficulty Strongsoul found the way
to the courtyard. There he addressed Saunders
very severely.

'I am ashamed of you,' he began ; but he got

no farther, for at that moment the fathers of the
pilgrims appeared and led them home.

Only the honorary steward and the honorary
porter were awake. The honorary secretary lay
with his head among the ruins of his pipe, and the
other two were crumpled up in their chairs like lay
figures.

The melancholy porter said, 'Strongsoul, of course,
was the son of Ninian Jamieson.'

'Oh!' said Cosmo, with a withering glance, 'that
actually occurs to you, does it?'

'When did this happen?' asked the timid steward
timidly.

'Last summer,' said Cosmo.

'But,' said the timid man still more timidly,
'there was no royal visit to the Duke of Moredun
last summer.'

'I've nothing to do with that. Young Jamieson
told a story to his father, his father told it to me,
and I have told it to you—for my own pleasure
entirely, observe you, not for yours. It would be
unbecoming in a Great Man to endeavour to enter-
tain others. Secretary, do your duty,' said Cosmo,
shaking that official roughly.

The honorary secretary started up, his hair

powdered with the ashes of his pipe, and fragments of pipeclay sticking all over his face. Mechanically he took out his watch, seized his tumbler, and muttered in a sleepy voice, 'This stated meeting of the Great Men is at an end.'

Printed by R. & R. CLARK, *Edinburgh.*

www.ingramcontent.com/pod-product-compliance
Lightning Source LLC
Chambersburg PA
CBHW031405020726
47499CB00005B/1478